Say You Won't Go

JM Dragon & Erin O'Reilly

Say You Won't Go

JM Dragon & Erin O'Reilly

Affinity
eBook Press
NZ
2017

Say You Won't Go
© 2017 by JM Dragon & Erin O'Reilly

Affinity E-Book Press NZ LTD
Canterbury, New Zealand

2nd Edition

ISBN: 978-0-947528-71-3

Editor: CK King
Proof Editor: Alexis Smith
Cover Design: Irish Dragon Designs

ACKNOWLEDGMENTS

As always, we'd like to thank the team at Affinity Rainbow Publications for all the amazing things they contribute to the creation of our eBooks.

Irish Eyes, thank you for the great cover creation.

The editing team is outstanding. CK, your guidance and encouragement makes the editing process seamless and a learning experience. Alexis, thank you for proof reading for it is a learning experience too. Lisa, what would we do without your eye for detail and ferreting out those pesky typos.

Alice, thank you for all of your contributions and the creation of the eBook formats.

Lastly, thank you to all our loyal readers who continue to read our stories and keep encouraging us to write more as a team and individually.

DEDICATION

For all the Affinity Rainbow Publications authors.
Together we rock!

TABLE OF CONTENTS

ALSO BY JM DRAGON

Jeager's
Breaking the Silence
The Promise
Do Dreams Come True?
The One
Letting Go
Circus
Falling into Fate
The Fix-it Girl
In Name Only
Death is Only the Beginning
Lonely Angel
Echo's Crusade
A Window in Time
Waterfalls, Rainbows, and Secrets
The Dragon's Halloween Collection
Incantations – A Collaboration
Affinity's Christmas Collection 2010
Christmas Collection 2011
Christmas Collection 2012
Christmas Collection 2014
Define Destiny Series

Define Destiny Series
Haunting Shadows
In Pursuit of Dreams
Actions and Consequences
All Our Tomorrows
Two Steps Forward One Back
A World of Change

When Hell Meets Heaven Series
When Hell Meets Heaven
Fatal Hesitation

With Erin O'Reilly
Against All Odds
Take Me as I am
Echoes of the Past
The End Game
Requiem
Earthbound
New Beginnings
Atonement

ALSO BY ERIN O'REILLY

Specter of Fear
Next Time
Ready for Love
Return to Me
If I Were a Boy
Through the Darkness
Deception
Fearless
'55 Ford
Fractured
That Kiss
Revelations
Wolf at the Door
Sandcastles

When Hell Meets Heaven Series
Echoes of the Past
Paradox of Love
The End Game
Requiem

CHAPTER ONE

"God, what a dump. I hate this place." Taryn Donovan scowled. At twenty-four, she was feeling trapped. She spent most every day of her life in the same place and the same town, seeing the same faces day after day. Even her job as a waitress in the only restaurant in town was a hand-me-down from her mother who still worked part time at the tavern. What she'd give to feel the wind at her back as she escaped from the confines of her life.

She lived a misfit's life. If anyone paid her any attention in school she was often the butt of jokes and lewd comments, because of her father. Most of the time, she remained invisible while envying the popular kids who the teachers always called on first. They called her last, if at all. If any of them ever came into the Bourne Falls Tavern, they'd not look at her when they ordered, acting as if she didn't exist. The only ones who paid her any attention were the afternoon drunks who always tried to cop a feel, which she found revolting. The one positive out of it all was the thick skin she developed over the years, although if she were truthful, it did hurt.

1

Taryn wiped a damp cloth across the scarred, wooden table then used it on the vinyl bench seats of the booth. Lunch was over, and she made her way to the couple sitting at the only occupied table. "Can I get you folks anything else? More tea?"

"No, we're all set," the man said.

Taryn knew them. How couldn't she? Bourne Falls was a one-horse town on the edge of nowhere. She made it a rule never to call any of the customers by name. Now, she faced Ruben and Ada Blankenship who both had taught at the high school. He taught chemistry and she English Lit. Ada was a stout woman with snow-white hair braided around the top of her head. Ruben was a big man with a comb over that looked more like peach fuzz than hair.

"Here you go. Keep the change." Ruben handed her a twenty. It would cover the bill and give her a one dollar and twenty-five cent tip.

"Thanks." She walked the money over to Burt, the day bartender. In a little over forty minutes, happy hour would start for the day drinkers. She wasn't looking forward to that. She'd seen every drunk in town at one time or another. It wasn't a pretty sight. She cleared the last table and looked around to make sure everything was ready.

"Here you go, honey." Rosie, the cook, passed her a ham and cheese sandwich through the kitchen window. "Seemed like we had more of a crowd today for lunch. I almost ran out of the special."

"Thanks." Taryn took the offered plate. "Yeah, all those hands from the Circle D came in at once, and they each tipped me a buck."

"Gonna make you rich." Rosie laughed. "Beef stew is the dinner special. I'd better go give it a stir."

Taryn set her plate on a table and slouched into a chair. "This place sucks," she muttered before taking a bite of her sandwich. It wasn't long before she heard the door bang shut and looked up expecting to see one of the day drinkers—most likely Hank Meadows—come sauntering in.

†

The sound of a pig squealing for the thousandth time made Logan Perry grind her teeth, as she punched at the aircon button for the tenth time. *I'm damn boiling, what's going on here?* She shook her head and saw a sign for a town. *Bourne Falls.* "Come on, girl, you can make it, I know you can." She caressed the wheel, hoping this town in the middle of nowhere had a decent mechanic.

Fifteen minutes later and feeling like her body was on fire, she parked outside a building predictably signed *Bourne Fall's Garage.* A boy—he looked barely eighteen—greeted her, wiping his hands on a greasy cloth. *I only thought they did that in the movies. How bizarre.*

"What can I do for you?"

"Shelia is in trouble, no air con and she's squealing like a stuck pig." Logan placed a protective hand on the hood.

The kid shrugged. "Sounds like it needs a fan belt."

Logan towered within inches of the mechanic and snarled, "Shelia is not an *it*. Got me?"

The boy cowered. "Yeah, yeah."

"Good. Can you fix her?"

"Yye…yes, two hours max," the boy stuttered.

"That long? Damn." She glanced at her watch. Almost two. "Recommend anywhere to eat?"

"The Tavern, it's the best in town."

Logan nodded, then turned to exit the building. "Where is this place?"

"Can't miss it. Two hundred yards down Main Street."

3

Minutes later, Logan curled her lip as she approached the local tavern, unimaginatively named after the town. She glanced around, noting the peeling, green paint of the wooden exterior and several small windows, which were dark, almost black. *Maybe they need a good cleaning. Inviting? Hardly.* The only thing that had made her stop here was that her beloved 1993 Ford Ranger needed a new fan belt. So, here she was in front of the establishment and walking toward the entrance. A dog-eared menu, plastered on the cracked wooden door, greeted her. "Nice welcome." She gave the menu a cursory read and pushed open the door. *I'm here, so let's see if the hick boy knows what he's talking about or if I'm going to reduce his bill.*

Logan perused the inner sanctum and laughed, uncaring if anyone noticed. The expression *inner sanctum* always made her laugh. She attributed it to religion, and there was no way she was religious. Not in this lifetime anyway. Appearing to be the only patron, she wondered how long it would take for someone to notice her. Her eyes scanned the dimly lit place, noting the waitress appeared to be having a break. *That boy is going to pay.*

Sitting at the nearest table, the cleanliness surprised her. Even though she knew what was on it, she picked up the menu—selections as bland as the name of the tavern. Her attention diverted from the menu to the movement of the waitress. She scrunched her eyes and inwardly grinned. *Nice.*

No one ever came into Bourne Falls Tavern that didn't live in the town or its outskirts. Taryn shook her head. Her eyes traced the body of a woman with shoulder length, white-blonde hair. Wearing jeans and a tight-fitting tank top, she stood at the door and looked around. *Wow, a stranger. Wonder what she's doing here?* The sandwich forgotten, excitement at speaking to someone new rushed through her body before she slid out of her chair. *The day is definitely looking up.*

Taryn stopped in midstride toward the new arrival. No one had ever looked at her the way the stranger was. The woman obviously hadn't gotten the memo that Taryn was invisible, since she seemed to be undressing her with her eyes. A shiver ran through her body, as she forced herself to move forward. Once she arrived at the table, the woman's emerald green eyes captured her and suspended life for a moment.

"What can I get for you?"

"Well, I can think of a lot of things, but I'm sure you meant from the menu."

Taryn blushed and stammered, "Cc…can I get you something to drink while you decide?"

The woman stared at her then glanced down at the menu. "Black coffee and water, thanks."

"You got it." As Taryn walked away, she swore she could feel the woman's eyes on her and when she glanced back, the woman winked. *Shit, what's that all about?* At the coffee station, she poured a cup of the dark brew and filled a glass with ice and water before heading back to the table. "Here you go. Decided on what you want yet?

"Just the way I like it…hot." The woman smiled slowly, as her lips caressed the edge of the cup. "Any recommendations?"

Taryn swallowed hard when she saw the woman lick her lips. Suddenly her body began reacting in a strange way, and she felt herself squirm. "Well…hmm," she stuttered, "the burgers are good."

Slim fingers with short, well-manicured fingernails tapped the menu. "You choose the type of burger for me and we will see how good they are. I trust you." She grinned.

"Oh, okay." That surprised Taryn, as it wasn't often that anyone asked her opinion on anything, not even the randy ranch hands. *I think she's flirting with me. No, that can't be.* Taryn didn't really have any frame of reference for thinking that, but somehow, she knew it was true. She giggled.

"Is it that good?"

Flustered, Taryn only nodded and walked toward the kitchen window. "A burger with everything, Rosie."

"Who's the stranger?"

"No idea."

"Want fries with that?"

"Sure, why not. She told me to choose."

"Whoa, I like the sound of that. She might be a live one, and you know we could do with that around here, big time."

"That we could."

Taryn's eyes fell on the stranger who was openly staring at her. She looked away when the sound of the door opening drew her attention. "Is it happy hour already?" She frowned as two of the town's drunks entered.

Logan enjoyed the mild flirting with the waitress. She appeared naïve but was a definite looker. Smoldering brown eyes with a little-girl-lost expression always appealed to her. Her body wasn't like a stick, either, with plenty of curves in all the right places. *Hmm wouldn't mind copping a feel of those breasts.* She licked her lower lip at the thought then let out a sigh.

Her attention turned to the loud voices of the two men that had just entered. They were, she decided, in their mid-thirties with heavily bristled faces, wearing clothes that looked like they needed laundering. *Gross. How the hell can any woman think that is attractive?* She diverted her attention to the waitress who was heading in the direction of the two men. *Now that's what I call attractive.*

Picking up her coffee, she overtly watched their exchange and it grossed her out again when the taller of the men tried to grope the waitress who grimaced and pulled away. *Good for her.*

"Taryn, come on, give me that kiss you're always promising me." Logan heard the smaller man say. The woman politely rebuffed him by shaking her head and retreating around the counter. *Good move.*

"You're gutter crap. Don't know why I bother. Our usual two beers and don't expect a tip."

At the derogatory remark, Logan moved upwards in her chair grasping her arms with fingers like limpets that prevented her body from moving toward the men. "Assholes," she muttered. Settling herself back down in the chair, she gulped on the cooling coffee before replacing the cup on the table.

"Want a refill?"

She saw a cheerful smile. "Thanks."

"You're welcome. Your burger won't be long." The tinkle of a bell had her nodding. "There it is now."

"Thanks." Logan watched as Taryn sashayed away. At least she now knew the name of this attractive woman. *Maybe she swings my way.* Glancing at her watch and grimacing, she sighed. *Even I don't have time to make that kind of conquest.* The more she thought of it, the more it irritated her that she didn't have the time.

Taryn placed the plate on the table and smiled. "Hope you like it."

"I'm sure I will. I see you do those curly fries, my favorite." The woman picked up a fork and placed one in her mouth.

Feeling completely out of her element, Taryn knew her face was red. In all the years she'd worked at the Tavern no one, except for the drunks, paid her much attention. And that was fine with her. "I took a chance that you'd want fries." She held her breath as she watched the woman take a bite and let it out when she smiled.

"Excellent choice. Are you the only person working today, other than the cook?"

"Well, there's Burt, the bartender. We get another waitress for the dinner crowd." She couldn't help looking at the woman's face. "Whatcha doin' in town? We don't get many strangers."

The woman scratched the side of her mouth then smiled. "Car trouble. How good is the mechanic in town? He said Shelia would be ready in two hours."

"Shelia, your car's name is Shelia? Sounds like a great name for a vehicle." Taryn grinned. "I guess you took your car to Bourne Falls Garage. Tommy is the mechanic, but I can't tell you much. I don't own a car." She shrugged. "A bike is my transportation when I don't walk."

"A bike huh? I haven't ridden one since I was in high school, used to be fun. If I had the time, I'd ask you if you wanted company on a bike ride to show me around town." The woman wriggled her eyebrows.

Taryn opened her mouth, but the words wouldn't come out. She now was sure that the woman was flirting with her. She took a deep breath and said, "Are you in a big hurry? I was thinking of going down to the old swimming hole for a dip later." She held her breath again.

"Sounds interesting, but I have a room booked in St. Louis, and it's too late to change the booking without getting charged for the room. Although, I am tempted." She took a bite of the burger and grease slipped out onto her chin.

Taryn held out her hand. "My name is—"

Wiping away the grease from her chin, the woman rose and took the offered hand. "Taryn, I know. I heard the guys over there call you by name. I'm Logan."

"Hmm, that's a pretty name." Taryn grinned. "So, you're tempted…what about going with me to swim?"

"Unless your break is in the next hour, I'm sorry. Maybe next time I come around this way I'll stay longer."

Taryn frowned. "Oh, okay."

Just then, Tommy McGill entered the tavern and came to stand nervously next to her. "Hmm, about your car…hmm…it isn't just the fan belt…. The compressor in the air conditioning unit. It needs replacing."

"And that's a problem?" The woman's reply was stern.

"Hmm, well I have to send away for the part. Your vehicle is old, and we don't have the part in stock. I'll have to send for it."

Logan stood in front of Tommy, who was sweating profusely. "How long, a couple of hours, half a day, what?"

"Well, it's Friday, and the fastest we could get the part here is Tuesday." He took a step back to stand behind Taryn.

"Just perfect, absolutely perfect," Logan hissed. She looked at Taryn, who gave her a small smile. "Tuesday morning by ten the latest."

Tommy nodded and shot out of the Tavern.

"Is that invitation for a bike ride and a swim still available?"

"Oh, yes, and there isn't a motel for at least thirty miles, so you can stay with me." She shrugged. "And Brenda. If you want?"

"Brenda?"

"My mother."

"Oh. Well that's an invitation I'm not going to ignore, thank you. When do you get off work?"

"After the dinner crowd thins out. Usually around six-thirty." Taryn laughed. "They all come for the early bird special."

Logan winked. "Guess I'll be back for dinner too then. Want to join me when you finish your shift?"

Taryn could feel her insides turn to mush. *Is this what falling for someone feels like?* She shook her head at the absurd thought. "I'd love to."

"Wonderful. Now, I'd better eat this burger before it gets cold. I have to say, it's delicious…good call."

With a blush, Taryn turned away when three more happy-hour men came into the tavern.

CHAPTER TWO

For some reason, it appeared that everyone in town had decided to come into the Tavern at the same time. She was so busy moving between tables that the only time she could pay attention to Logan was when she placed the bill on the table.

"Sorry I can't stay, I'm slammed. Do you mind paying at the bar?"

Logan's response was a wink, as she placed a twenty over the bill. "Keep the change." She stood and smiled. "See you later."

All Taryn could do was stare after Logan, who was disappearing out the door. In the brief time since she'd met Logan, Taryn couldn't keep her eyes off the woman. Every time she looked in her direction, she could feel a warm sensation coursing through her body. She couldn't remember a real person ever flirting with her, or for that matter, paying attention to her at all. Seven o'clock couldn't come fast enough.

Ten minutes later, Brenda arrived and Taryn went to her immediately. "I've invited someone to spend the weekend with us." She whipped off her apron and handed it to the woman. "I'm going outside for a breath of fresh air. All the tables have been served." As she turned to leave, Brenda grabbed her arm.

"Who?" Brenda gave her an incredulous look. "You've never had a guest in my home, much less someone to spend the night."

Taryn grinned. "Her car broke down, and it will take until Tuesday to fix. I told her she could stay with us." She lifted one shoulder. "You know there's no place to stay in Bourne."

"Oh," her mother said, sounding disappointed.

"Sorry, it's not a man." Taryn fixed Brenda with a glare. "That's your department, isn't it?"

"Wow, you've finally got an opinion. Next time, keep it to yourself."

I did, didn't I? Taryn smiled. *I think it's Logan giving me a backbone where Brenda is concerned.*

"We don't have a guest room, so she'll have to stay with you, and you'll buy her food. I don't have money to waste on strangers."

"That doesn't surprise me." With that, Taryn turned and walked toward the door with a small smile playing on her lips. *We'll be sharing a room.* The possibilities were endless.

†

It took Logan all of five minutes to walk down the main street. The town was in need of some TLC. A lick of paint would do wonders for most of the single-story buildings. Flowers in the empty planter boxes that lined both sides of the street would be beneficial and bring color to the place. She'd never actually stayed any length of time in a town like this, traveled through a few in the last couple of months of her trip but never stopped to take in the sights. Observing the derelict buildings, she knew now the reason. She passed what appeared to be the bank with metal guards over the windows and doors, and cream brickwork. *At least that's presentable.*

Hmm and I get to play with a local. I just wonder how worldly Taryn is…. Who cares? It will be fun. She softly chuckled.

The clearing of a throat behind her prompted her to swing around to see who it was. A man moved out of the shadow of the hardware store to her left and nodded.

"Sheriff, anything I can do for you?" Logan smiled slightly and watched the thin man raise bushy eyebrows in her direction. He raised a hand to his chin and pulled at it a couple of times.

"We don't often get visitors in town, are you just passing through?"

Logan considered the question for a moment then shrugged. "Was. Now, circumstances, as in my car needs repair, mean I'll be here until Tuesday."

"No motel in this town, are you sleeping in your car?" The sheriff narrowed his eyes, but his tanned features took on a friendlier look. At least Logan thought so.

"No, I've been fortunate to meet someone here, and she offered me a room at her house." The man shuffled forward, and Logan noticed that his shiny black shoes looked out of place in this drab town.

"Is that so. May I ask who that might be?"

Logan flexed her left hand several times, then pointed to the tavern. "The waitress there."

"Brenda?" He frowned heavily this time and looked less friendly.

Logan shook her head. "Nope, Taryn." A grin edged at her lips when the man's eyes bulged. "She was very kind."

Scratching his cheek, the sheriff shook his head. "Yep, I'm sure that Taryn is a kind woman. I'll let you be on your way. I guess you will have lots of things to do. If you get in any trouble, ask for me. The name is Sheriff Waltham." He turned back toward the hardware shop and went inside.

Logan didn't move. *That was different.* She looked around and decided to head back to the garage to collect a few of her things, namely her sneakers. It was a good day for a walk, and it would kill time until she had her rendezvous with the lovely Taryn. She grinned, then began to whistle one of her favorite tunes, "Crazy," as she headed back to the garage.

†

Taryn couldn't keep her eyes off the entrance, and when she saw Logan walk in the door, she thought her face would break from her smile. Taking off her apron, she walked quickly to her new friend. "Good, you're early."

Logan grinned. "When a lovely lady volunteers to show me around on her bike, with the chance of swimming with her afterwards, what do you expect? I'm ready, though I did ask you to have dinner with me."

Her smile widened. "Come on, you need to meet Brenda. I told her you'd be staying at the house and I…well, I think you should at least say 'hi' to her."

"Whoa, meeting Mom and we haven't even held hands yet."

Taryn couldn't help but laugh. "Didn't I tell you I'm kinda unconventional?"

Logan wriggled her eyebrows and winked. "Hmm unconventional and meeting Mom don't usually share the same sentence. However, I'm broad minded, so hey, let's go meet Mom."

14

After grabbing Logan's hand, Taryn took her over to the bar. "Brenda, this is the girl I was telling you about."

Brenda gave Logan a once over and shook her head. "Kinda fancy for the likes of here."

"Nice to meet you, Brenda, I'm Logan Perry." She held out her free hand.

Brenda snorted. "Fancy name too, where you from?"

"Chicago born and raised." Logan dropped her hand.

Taryn screwed up her face and held out her hand. "Gimme."

"Fine, but if you do anything I don't approve, you're out on your ear. Hear me?" She glared at both Taryn and Logan.

Taryn grabbed the keys from her hands and dragged Logan over to where Rosie was standing in the kitchen. "Is it ready?"

"Hold your horses, young lady. Ain't you gonna introduce me first?"

"Sorry, yes. Logan, this is Rosie, our cook." Her eyes widened. "Is it ready?"

"Rosie, pleased to meet you." Logan held out her hand.

For the first time ever, Taryn saw Rosie blush, as she took Logan's hand. "Pleased to meet you." She dropped the hand, lifted a basket, and set it on the counter. "Here you go, Taryn. Fried chicken and the works."

"Likewise." Logan smiled, shaking her head.

Taryn grabbed the basket in one hand and Logan's hand in the other. "Come on, our chariot awaits."

"Do you need me to carry that basket? It looks heavy."

Taryn grinned and shook her head, as she pulled them closer to the door.

Logan disengaged her hand and opened the door.

Taryn followed. "Thanks."

"My pleasure, especially as I get to have a picnic too. How did you guess it was one of my favorite things to do?"

"I…I guessed." Taryn was shaking inside. *What an idiot going to all this trouble for a stranger. What was I thinking? More to the point, what will she think?* "Come on." She led them down the street to the side of the wooden building. "Close your eyes." She watched as Logan complied, then led her by the hand toward the parking lot at the back of the Tavern. "Okay, open them." The look on Logan's face as she took in the cherry-red '67 GTO was worth it all.

"Oh my god, you have a classic car?" She turned to Taryn.

"Hmm, it was my dad's and his dad's before him…now it's Brenda's." She shrugged. "He's dead, and Brenda is the town slut." She refused to look at Logan, as she unlocked the door. "Still want to have a picnic and a swim?" *Probably not.*

Logan saw the embarrassment, or maybe shame, on Taryn's face, as she spoke the words damning her mother. Life was never easy; it had its ups and downs, that was for sure. This was a little bit more noticeable in the Tavern. The question was, did she want to enter into the mix. She looked at the downcast face of her new friend, who had made such a wonderful effort for a virtual stranger. *Sure, I do.*

"Hey, are you old enough to drive this beauty? I'd be quite happy to volunteer. I love older cars. You can be assured that I will take great care. Does she have a name?" Her hand traced over the smooth paint work. Logan smiled, as Taryn slowly looked up with a tentative expression on her face. "Is that a maybe?"

"I'm old enough. It's Brenda's pride and joy. I think she loves this car more than me." Taryn shrugged.

"I doubt it. Let me tell you, from someone who cherishes their vehicle more than another person, no way would she have given you the keys. She must love you." Logan opened the passenger door and slid in. The leather seats felt wonderful. It was a truly cherished vehicle.

Sliding into the driver's seat and closing the door, Taryn smiled. "I remember her baking cookies and smiling all the time before my dad died. Then she changed. So you know, I had to take one of her shifts so I could use it." Taryn chewed on her lip and frowned. "Enough of that. Let's go have some fun."

Logan reached across and placed her hand on Taryn's as she was about to insert the key. "Fun sounds great to me. Can we have the fried chicken as well?"

Taryn winked, started the car, and pulled out of the parking lot. "If you insist, but I think we need to swim first and eat later. Don't you? The sun will only be out for another hour and a half or so." She maneuvered the car a little way out of town.

"Yeah, sure, I forgot about the swim…well not really forgot, exactly. You said skinny dipping right, because I didn't come prepared." She wriggled her eyebrows.

"Well, not exactly skinny dipping, I usually wear my underwear." She shrugged. "Is that okay?"

"Of course, it is."

"I've never taken anyone to my swimming hole 'cause…well let's just say I don't have anyone other than Rosie as a friend." She shrugged. "I pretty much keep to myself and have never been particularly popular."

"Why? You are lovely to look at and have a kind heart. Who wouldn't want to know you?" Logan frowned. "Well, I like you and the others can go to hell… It's hot, even at six

17

forty-five, so I say let's get our skin wet. Are you with me?" Logan smiled. This woman was a contradiction but interesting. "Are we there yet?'

"Couple more minutes, I promise." Taryn desperately wanted to have eye contact with Logan. Those emerald, sparkling eyes drew her, but she had to concentrate or they would end up in a ditch and Brenda would kill her. She giggled. She turned onto a dirt road and followed it for a hundred yards, before trees engulfed the car, making it seem to disappear. Taryn put her foot to the brake pedal, making the tires skid along the weeds and leaving a plume of dust behind them. "We're here."

"Then it must be time to get wet." Logan winked at her.

"Sure, let's get it on." She grinned and pulled off her shirt. "I can feel the cool water already."

"You are one crazy girl, but I love that. Have you heard the song "Crazy" by Aerosmith? It reminds me of you right this minute." Logan chuckled and threw off her tank top. She glanced down at the expanse of tanned skin she showed to the world, nude-colored sports bra the only thing protecting her from true mother nature.

"God, I love that song. Have you seen the video?"

"One of my all-time favs. If we need to dress up at any time, I want to wear the tie." Logan chuckled.

"That's okay, I always fancied being a pole dancer. No chance of that in this town, not unless I want to get arrested."

"Hmm-um I don't know…the Sheriff didn't seem too intimidating."

Taryn took her eyes off the path for a few seconds, as she stared at her new friend. "You've met Sheriff Waltham? Why? Did you do something wrong?"

Logan burst out laughing. "Well, if staying in town for a few days is wrong, then I guess."

"I don't think so. He was a friend of my dad's...they worked together."

"He was a cop?"

"Yes, but I didn't know him very well...he died when I was five."

"I'm sorry. My parents are alive and kicking in Vermont...they love to ski."

"Oh, are you rich then?" Taryn's heart did a double flip at that piece of information, she was hardly friend material for a rich girl.

"Nah, Dad is a security guard, and Mom is a sales clerk."

Taryn pointed at the water. "What do you think?"

"Wow, look at the shimmer in the water. It's like a mirror image pool. The trees look real in the water." Logan climbed out of the car and strode to the edge of the swimming hole.

Taryn began chewing on her fingers and shaking her head. "Whose great idea was this? I can't believe I'm here with her," she muttered.

"Hey, you mumbling to yourself over there, or are you going to take in this fabulous view with me?" Logan turned and smiled.

"Sorry. Like I said, I've never brought anyone here before...I almost forgot you." Taryn smiled. "Almost"— Taryn grinned, pointing to a rope— "see that rope over there?"

Logan removed her gaze from Taryn, looking in the direction indicated, and nodded.

"It took me most of a day, but I got it hanging there. Then it took me a week to get up the nerve to swing on it."

"I'm impressed, since you're such a small thing…. I guess small in stature but tall in courage."

"Yeah, right. Anyway, one day when I thought I was taking a shortcut, I got lost and found this place. I fell in love with it instantly. Something about the stillness called to me, and it's been my special place ever since."

"Mine too, now. I'm a city girl and live in Chicago. The nearest I'd get to this kind of experience is in my dreams." Logan reached out and clutched Taryn's hand. "Thank you for allowing me to share this special place with you."

Taryn could feel the heat on her cheeks, and that made her blush even more. "Wow, it's gotten hot. Are you ready to swim?" She slipped off her pants. "Last one in is a rotten egg," she said with a laugh before running toward the water. Wading in, she stood watching and waiting.

"Hey, no one beats me," Logan shouted after taking off her jeans and splashing into the water.

Taryn couldn't take her eyes off the partially clad woman taking long strides toward her through the water. Logan's body was unbelievably toned, with an all-over tan. "Oh, my god, she is stunning." The nearer Logan got to her, the more heat Taryn could feel spreading through her body. Never in her life had she experienced such a feeling. Finally, Logan was standing in front of her, and Taryn shook her head and splashed water toward her.

"Ah, a playful puppy. Well, see what you think about this." Logan's hand skimmed the surface of the water, and then with a curve of her hand, flicked water into Taryn's face.

"Oh, you." Taryn swam away. "Try and catch me," she taunted when she reached the deeper water. Her eyes fixated on the body that swam toward her, but as Logan came within a foot of her, she swam away in the opposite direction. It was going to take an accomplished swimmer to catch her…unless of course she wanted to be caught. She grinned as Logan came at her again, and she diverted toward the rope.

"Hey, anyone ever called you Mermaid before?"

Taryn shook her head as she smiled. "Not until today. Why? Do you give up, since you can't catch me?"

"Sure, I can."

Logan swam toward her strongly. *She's better than I expected for a city girl, but I'm better.* The warm sensation in her stomach at that thought made her happy. It was the first time she had ever compared herself to someone else and come out on top. Maybe Logan wouldn't agree, but this was a good thing.

"See, told you so. You can't catch me. Want to try the rope swing?" Taryn burst out laughing at the incredulous expression on Logan's face. "What are you, chicken? Don't you like heights?"

"Heights ain't what I'm afraid of, rope burns are. We haven't many clothes on, remember."

"Well, if you do it right, you'll never get a rope burn. Want me to teach you?" After Logan nodded, Taryn swam toward the shore, got out, and headed to the rope wrapped around a large tree branch. "Come on, Logan."

"Okay, now what?"

"Easy. First you put both feet on the big knot, then you stand, wrap both hands around the upper rope, and begin to swing. Once you're far enough out, you let go." She saw the doubt on Logan's face. "Here, let me show you." Taking the rope, she expertly climbed on, and soon she was swinging out over the water. She let go.

Logan watched Taryn carefully climb up the rope and do exactly what she'd described. *Damn, she's one hot woman.* Her lithe body had small, barely a handful breasts, which were pert. Logan imagined the nipples light brown, and her mouth salivated at the thought of sucking them and bringing them to attention. As Taryn swung on the rope, her hips swayed, and Logan could see what she thought was silky, pale hair peeking out of her underwear. *My god this woman is driving me crazy. She definitely has no inhibitions. And she says no one likes her. What are they putting in the water here? No surprise it's a dying town.*

"Are you chicken?" Taryn's voice skimmed off the water.

Logan sucked in a breath, headed for the rope, and climbed just as instructed. She yelled as she let go, splashing into the water with a force that was less than she'd expected. "I'm here, now what?"

Taryn laughed, swam toward her, and grabbed her gently by neck. "Wanna to go again?"

Logan twisted out of the grip and placed her hands on Taryn's shoulders. "Care to have a wager?" Brown eyes stared into hers, and the skin at the side of Taryn's eyes crinkled for a second before they smoothed away.

"A wager, huh? What'd ya have in mind?"

Logan moved her head from side to side as she took in the fresh-faced woman who, in Chicago, in her circles, would be sought after. "If I can get farther in the water than you…within three goes, you let me drive the car. If you win, you get to name your prize."

"You're on. I'll even let you go first." Taryn grinned.

"You never said what prize you wanted. Not that it matters." Logan winked and grabbed the rope. "I'm going to get to drive that car for sure."

"Don't count those chickens just yet," Logan heard Taryn call out, just as she let go of the rope.

†

The bright green and lime foliage from the tall poplar trees which surrounded the swimming hole made an excellent hedge to give them privacy should anyone pass by. Not that anyone ever did, according to Taryn. Still, Logan decided that the shadiest part of the area, which also included a large, flat stone big enough for both of them to share, was prudent as they were still scantily clad after the swim.

The basket of fried chicken, salad, water, and soda was just the thing after the boisterous antics of trying to outdo each other on the rope swing. *I haven't had that much fun since I was in middle school.* The original wager was based on three rounds, but they were having such a good time they ended up taking six turns each. Taryn won by one. *Hmm I wonder what she wants as payment. She hasn't said yet.* Logan poked her hand into the basket and withdrew a drumstick and bit it with relish. Grease began to dribble down her chin. Leaning over, she tried and failed to stop the offending moisture from trickling down between her breasts. "Damn."

"Guess that chicken is juicy." Taryn cleared her throat and looked away, apparently trying to stifle a chuckle.

"Yeah, yeah, yeah. Did Rosie pack napkins?" Logan rummaged in the basket, but Taryn's hand touched hers, stopping her motions.

"Would you like some help with that?"

Logan grinned. "Absolutely, ma'am." She watched Taryn lean into the basket and felt the brush of a shoulder along her stomach. A tingle went up Logan's spine at the close proximity.

Taryn suddenly held several napkins aloft and waved them at Logan. Clearing her throat, Taryn visibly shivered. "I think you can wipe it off yourself…can't you?" She looked away.

Now, there is an interesting conundrum. Dare I ask? Maybe it's a little too early. "I'm a big girl and I can manage, but thanks for the offer." Logan took a napkin and squeezed Taryn's hand. "Going to share what you want for the wager you won? I'm dying to know."

Taryn looked at her with a crooked smile. "Well, I think, if it is okay with you, I'd like you to come back here with me tomorrow after I get off work." Her face looked hopeful. "What do you say? I'll even throw in a short drive of the GTO."

"You mean I have to go without the pleasure of your company when I get up in the morning? Damn, that's hard." Logan pulled at her chin and then smiled. "You got it. Believe me, it's one of the best wagers I've lost in a long time. I usually have to give up my shirt."

"I'll save that one for later, when you lose to me again." Taryn plopped a spoonful of salad on her plate. "That is, if you aren't chicken." She wiggled her eyebrows.

Logan shook her head. "With you, I'm game for anything. This chicken, I have to say, is delicious, definitely not 'Kentucky' recipe." She snagged another piece and bit into it.

"So, if you're from Chicago, why in the world are you here in Bumfuck, Nowhere?"

"Bumfuck, Nowhere, wow." Logan laughed. "My mom would have boxed my ears if I called Chicago that. Does your mother know you say things like that?" Logan dropped the chicken and gazed at Taryn.

"Brenda has the mouth of a sailor, so no, she won't care what I say." She shrugged. "Actually, she doesn't pay me any attention, which I don't mind at all. I can come and go as I please."

Logan took one of Taryn's hands in hers and squeezed gently. "You really hate this town and even your mother. So why not leave?"

Taryn bit out a sarcastic laugh. "Where would I go on my bike? I barely make enough money to get a new pair of shoes every six months, and in my job, that is a necessity. At least here, I have a place to live, even if it's with Brenda who charges me for the privilege."

The vitriol that came from such lovely looking lips amazed Logan. *I'm a hypocrite, I hated my parents for a while when they moved to Vermont without me. Guess that makes us even.* "My gran died a year ago, and she left me two hundred and fifty thousand dollars. She told me to spend it all in two years or she was going to rise from the dead and make my life hell."

A hand threw over Taryn's mouth. "You're kidding me, right?"

Logan shook her head.

"Two hundred and fifty thousand dollars…you're rich. I can't even fathom having money like that. Wow. You are not going to spend it all, are you?"

Crouching on the stone, her hands wrapped around her knees, Logan shrugged. "My gran was half Cherokee, she didn't believe in leaving things behind not to use. I guess a part of her still lives in me. Shelia was the only actual possession I had. I rented an apartment and had a dumb job as a call center operator. Gran's bequest came at the right time I guess. I'm thirty-two, and I want to see more of the country. Do you think that's bad, wasting my inheritance on a trip?"

"No, I don't think so. I envy you being able to do that. Will your job still be there when you get done touring around?" Taryn blew out a breath. "If it were me, I'd run away to Hollywood."

"Hollywood? Do you dream of being an actress?"

Taryn laughed. "No. Growing up, we'd see people come through town carrying a suitcase and heading west. My granny would tell me they were heading for Hollywood to become stars." She chuckled. "I think I was nine before I realized she wasn't serious."

"Hollywood isn't all it's cracked up to be if you look at the stats of hopefuls and what they end up doing. You know what I'd love to run? My own café. Sounds dumb I guess, but I make a mean cup of coffee. I'd need someone to orchestrate the food and stuff, but there is money in it. That's my dream."

"Hey, that's a fantastic dream. I'd come to work for you."

Logan turned and briefly touched Taryn's cheek. "We'd make a fantastic team." She gazed into the brown eyes for a few seconds longer. "Okay, it's getting chilly out here. What's for dessert?" She stood.

"Well, this isn't much of a dessert kinda town, but Rosie put some of her homemade, double fudge brownies in the basket for us. What do you say we go back to my house and have our dessert after we get you settled in?" She winked. "Promise you won't be disappointed."

Logan held out a hand. "After today, nothing will disappoint me." Taryn rose, taking the offered hand. They were inches away from each other, and the warm breath on her body incited more in Logan than she wanted to admit. *I like this woman. She's worth getting to know.* "Let's go. Can't wait to see where you live."

CHAPTER THREE

Taryn navigated the car to a smallish house in need of repair. The front porch was missing parts of the floor, and the screen door hung precariously to one side. *What a dump. I can't believe I'm bringing Logan here.* She turned the car off and shrugged. "Here we are. Not much, but it's better than sleeping on the street." Embarrassment filled her when she saw Logan scrunch up her face. "I'm sure you're used to better places to live."

"I really appreciate this, Taryn. To be honest, the thought of spending the night...no, three nights in that garage wasn't exactly appealing, even though I love Shelia. I'd even sleep out on your porch...you have a magnificent view of the mountains."

Taryn shook her head. "You're amazing. Are you always so laid back? You seem to just go with whatever comes along."

Logan grinned. "Told you, I'm part Indian. We have the chill factor down to an art. My great-grandmother used to sit in the corner of the room and lose herself 'to the heavens'

27

she used to say. I personally think she was having a nana nap."

Taryn couldn't help laughing. "She sounds like someone I'd like to know. Well, come on, I'll show you where you'll be staying for the next few days. She opened the door and sighed—Brenda had actually cleaned the house—it didn't look so bad. "This is home sweet home," she said sarcastically. "I spend as little time as possible here." Taryn watched for any expression of distaste as Logan entered the house. There wasn't any, just a calmness that made her look beautiful.

"I love the smell of beeswax; it gives that homely feeling. It's larger inside than I expected." Logan smiled.

"When my dad died, Brenda didn't want to live on the farm anymore. One day, she just packed up all our belongings and moved to town to live with her mother, leaving my dad's parents to run the farm alone." She looked around. "Come on, I'll show you to my room. It's kinda small…" Taryn didn't look at Logan and headed down the narrow hallway, passing the first door then opening the second, and waved Logan inside.

"Wow you have an eye for color," Logan said. "Where did you get those pieces of artwork from? Thought you said you had no money? They would be worth a fortune in the city. Metal artwork is the new craze." Logan dropped her bag, and Taryn watched her pick up a colorful metal pig, about the size of an iPad. "Who made this?"

"Um, I did." Taryn lifted a shoulder. "My gramps was a blacksmith, and there's a shed out back where he used to make horseshoes for people. When I was in high school, I took a metal-working course." She shook her head. "It was the one thing I excelled at in school. I made myself a workshop of sorts in that shed."

28

"You are one talented girl, Taryn. Have you shown these to anyone, like an art dealer maybe?" Logan turned and gave her a huge smile.

"Thanks, but I doubt anyone would want to buy them. I just do it to keep myself busy while Brenda entertains. I was lucky that my teacher gave me the school's old welder when they got a new one."

Logan moved closer and took hold of her chin. "One thing my grandmother used to say was never give up until you tried something at least once. If you really want something, then you might need to try more than once."

"Oh, really…is there anything in particular you really wanted that you didn't try or tried more than once?"

Logan dropped her hand and shrugged. "About six years ago, I was in a relationship that kept falling apart. No matter how much I tried to make it work, things always went wrong. She called me too easy going and said I didn't care enough to make an effort for her. I guess some things just aren't meant to be."

I knew it! Taryn could feel her body shiver, as she recalled the moment that Logan ran her eyes up and down her body when she took her shorts off at the swimming hole. Bumfuck didn't have anyone that was gay, or at least no one admitted it…she hadn't. "Maybe she wasn't the right person for you. Did you ever think of that?"

"Sure, it hurt though. I decided there and then that in the future I'd keep my heart intact. What about you, any handsome lover in your skeleton cupboard?"

"Ha. Are you serious? Have you looked around this town and the people here? The only interesting person ever…is you." Taryn held her breath, wanting but not wanting, to hear Logan reply that she'd rather stay in her car.

"Well in that case, for the extent of my stay, you can have me as an attentive partner." Logan winked and moved closer to the bed.

"Does that mean we might hold hands?" She grinned. "Eyes will be popping out all over town." Taryn moved a little closer until their shoulders touched. "I've never had an 'attentive partner.' Sounds like fun."

"Then fun it shall be." Logan winked. "If you don't care about the townsfolk, I'm definitely not worried. Although, you should remember that I'll be gone in a few days, and you live here."

"Do you have any idea how long I've waited for you to come along? I've never cared what they think, 'cause they all act like I'm invisible." She grinned. "I can't wait to see their faces when we walk down the street holding hands." She gave Logan a curious look. "Will you hang around the Tavern when I work too?"

"What are your shift times this weekend?"

"Actually, I only work tomorrow. The place is closed Sunday, and I have Monday off next week. I start at five thirty then get off at two but have to be back at four. Penance for using her car is taking Brenda's shift."

"Wow, that's some long day you'll have ahead of you, girl. Not sure I can make it for five thirty. I'll definitely arrive for breakfast, and we can have lunch together. How does that sound?"

"Great. Maybe we can go swimming again in the afternoon, before I need to go back. It's karaoke night and that brings out all the drunks and wanna-be singers." Taryn could feel her body heat up at the thought of seeing Logan partially clothed again.

"Great plan, and I'll organize the lunch." Logan placed a finger to Taryn's lips. "No argument, I might surprise you.

Now are you going to offer me a beer or something? It was thirsty work all that rope swinging."

"One thing we always have on hand is beer. Come on," Taryn reached out her hand, "let's sit out on the porch."

†

The night was balmy, filled with the smell of jasmine and honeysuckle, as Taryn and Logan sat on the front porch drinking beer. Old Mr. Barker strolled by, tugging along his Labrador, followed by Mrs. Webber and her daughter. They never gave the two women a look.

"See, I told you no one ever sees me, not even the dog." Taryn said.

"Odd people, even in my congested neighborhood, people give you the time of day. Even if it's just a smile or a nod." Logan lifted the bottle to her lips and drank more beer.

"You'd think it would be that way in small towns but not this one. They have certain ideas about people and don't ever change their minds." Taryn moved her chair closer and took Logan's hand. "Let's see if the next one notices."

Logan chuckled. "Okay, fine by me. I like holding your hand. Incidentally, why is this town so run down?"

"My dad was one of the sheriff's deputies, and one night he got a call about a break-in. When he got there, he found Tommy Reinhold inside the house. The kid was stoned out of his head and went for my dad...he had no choice but to shoot him. The Reinhold family owned the factory everyone worked at. After the shooting, they closed it down and moved away." Taryn shrugged. "Things went downhill from there. They all blamed my dad, and by association, me and Brenda."

A somber silence permeated the air.

"What happened to your dad?" Logan squeezed Taryn's hand gently.

"He had a heart attack and died." She looked away. "I think it was because he was so stressed over shooting Tommy. I was only five at the time, so all I know is what I've overheard others say."

"He must have been really young to have a heart attack, though I guess stress would do that. I'm sorry for your loss."

The noise of several voices drifted in the air, and they both looked at the four men walking down the street, beer bottles in hand and laughing.

"Well let's see if your ploy to get noticed works." Logan pulled Taryn closer so her head was touching her shoulder.

"Hmm, this is nice, and I really don't care if they notice." Taryn snuggled closer. "Thank you."

"Anytime."

The four men came in their line of sight, and one of them stopped. He was short and obese, with a pug nose and a straggly, unkempt beard. "Boys, take a look at what we have here." The three other men stopped and stared before shaking their heads and laughing loudly.

"Damn, always called you queer folk, Taryn, now we know it's true. Does your momma know?" They began pointing their beer bottles in the direction of the porch.

Taryn suddenly felt emboldened, and she took her opportunity when Logan turned toward her. Taryn kissed her.

"Want some company?" Roy Blankenship sneered before grabbing himself. "I got the equipment and she ain't."

"Oh, she has so much more than you'll ever have, Roy."

"You don't know what you're missin'." The man waved her off, before they all walked away shouting at the top of their voices, "Dykes in town, dykes in town."

"Won't that action get back to everyone in town, including your mom? I know you say you don't care, but this is a big step, Taryn."

Taryn frowned. "I really don't care...but I do care if they give you a hard time."

"Hey, it's okay. I'm good with it, thick skin and all, I just wanted you to know what this means. Coming out with a stranger who isn't going to be around for the long term is a huge step." Logan pursed her lips.

The words "isn't going to be around for long term" stabbed at Taryn's heart, but she smiled anyway. "From the day I first heard them calling me names, I haven't cared what anyone in this town thinks. I'm invisible, so no one will care. Like you, I have thick skin...this town requires it."

"No one is that invisible. They called you names, so you are not invisible. Those jerks *did* stop and say something, even if it wasn't complimentary. What will your mom say, because people like that love to tell tales?" Logan drank heavily from her bottle, apparently draining it. Taryn watched her clunk it down it in front of her on the floor of the porch.

"Brenda, doesn't care about me. She's always trying to hook me up with her 'gentlemen callers'." She shivered. "That is so gross. Besides, I like you and I really don't care what anyone says."

Logan stood and held out her hand. "Sounds good to me. Want to show me your etchings?" Logan wriggled her eyebrows. "I'm dying to see inside this workshop you have. It calls to my butch side."

Taryn took Logan's hand and grinned. "Sure, if you're up for it. You may spaz out when you see my arc welder."

She laughed and squeezed the hand and led them off the porch.

†

Logan entered the rickety-looking building, little more than a double garage and in need of repair like everything in this town. She was behind Taryn, and as the flickers of strip lighting illuminated the inside, she couldn't believe her eyes.

A box-like contraption, about double the size of a computer console, sat next to a wooden bench over six feet long with what looked like a stainless-steel top. Several gadgets, presumably tools of the trade, were neatly laid out. On the other side of the bench, several sheets of steel in differing sizes were propped against the wall.

In the far corner stood a small booth with numerous cans of paint next to it.

"Taryn, this place is great. I'd spend most of my time here too." Logan grinned as she twirled around, taking in the unfinished masterpieces.

"It's where I come to get away from the smells of the Tavern. I can do whatever I want here." She toed the ground. "I like to create things."

Logan placed a hand on her shoulder. "You do a wonderful job. I might be able to create a great coffee, but this is incredible. You know, you really need to think about showing your stuff to an agent. I'm damn sure there's a market for your creativity."

Taryn looked down then up again. "I've never showed it to anyone else before. Do you really think someone would want to buy any of it? Brenda calls it crap."

"Me for sure. When I set up my café I want you to do all the artwork, and you can sell them from my place...what do you say?" Logan walked over to the booth.

34

"Café? You're really going to have one? Will you need a waitress? Can I work for you?"

Logan laughed. "Well it's kind of still in its infancy, but yeah that's what I want to do. Gran said spend the money. I've used some for the trip but have enough left to get me started, I hope. That's another reason I travelled—to find a place I want to set up in."

"And?"

"How about I find a place first then we discuss working arrangements. Hell, it could be in Timbuktu." Logan chuckled as she checked out the different colored paint tins.

Taryn took a step and pulled Logan into a hug. "You've given me something that I never thought I'd have."

"Okay, I'm game. What's that?"

"Hope that one day I'd be able to get out of Bumfuck for good."

Logan held Taryn away and smiled. "Somehow or another, I think you will, Taryn. With or without my help. Right, I guess as you get up so early, it's time for bed. I've had a busy day too. I'm almost dead on my feet."

"Let's go then. You can use the bathroom first."

CHAPTER FOUR

Taryn woke with a start and smiled when she saw a sleeping Logan next to her. She let her head rest on the pillow, remembering the feel of Logan's arm around her in the night. For the first time she could remember, she felt safe and cared about because of that simple gesture. Her eyes took in the crane on the ceiling that she always looked at first thing in the morning. How she wished she had wings to fly away. *Was Logan being sincere when she told me that I had talent and should sell my creations? Could I really sell any of it?* Certainly not to anyone in Bourne Falls, but a bigger town had possibilities.

After another quick look at the woman sleeping next to her, she quietly got out of the twin bed and made her way to the bathroom. The day couldn't go fast enough for her. The highlights would be seeing Logan for breakfast, going swimming—Logan said she'd furnish their picnic, and then seeing her again at dinner. The down side would be spending the night serving drinks to drunks while they murdered songs at karaoke night. "Damn, I wish I hadn't made that deal with Brenda. Logan and I coulda spent the evening together," she mumbled as she left the bathroom. They did have all day Sunday and Monday. That thought made her stomach do a flip-flop, because after that Logan would be gone and she'd have to go back to the same old routine.

Taryn quietly dressed in her work uniform before fastening the apron around her waist. *God, I hate this.* Looking at the sleeping Logan, she sighed. *I need to make the most out of the next days before she leaves.* With that thought, she leaned down and kissed Logan's cheek. "See you later," she whispered before walking out of the room and closing the door softly behind her.

Walking down the hallway, she heard loud snoring coming from Brenda's room. *Wonder who she let screw her now.* The possibilities were endless. She was certain that every man in town plus all the hands from the Circle D Ranch had been in Brenda's bed at one time or another. Her mind flashed to the time one of the men had tried to force himself on her. Brenda came flying and hit him over the head with a whiskey bottle then gave her an evil look and screamed, "get your own men." After that, Taryn kept her door locked with a chair back jammed under the knob. Word must have gotten around, because no one ever tried her door again.

The warm summer air engulfed her, as she stepped out onto the porch. The thought of seeing Logan at breakfast made her smile, and she hastened her steps. Just the thought of seeing Logan at the Tavern made a pleasant feeling course through her body. "Today is going to be great."

†

Logan dragged the pillow over her head, as the drone of bees going about their business just outside the window invaded her peace and quiet. Didn't anyone tell them it was too early to go to work? It was barely daybreak. Opening one eye, she peered at the side table and then remembered this wasn't her bed or her room. She furtively glanced to her right. Crumpled sheets were the only evidence someone else had been beside her all night. Ah yes, the lovely Taryn, who had such an innocence of life it was almost infectious. Logan looked up at the ceiling and smiled. The younger woman's metal art was very good. *Pity she won't show the pieces to anyone who could help her realize her potential.* Her eyes took in the iridescent blues and pinks, highlighting a foot-long crane in flight so authentic, that for just a moment, you could believe it was real. She moved her gaze to the table and wondered where the alarm clock was. Surely Taryn would need one, getting up so early for her shift. She scrambled over to the other side of the bed. Low and behold, there was a clock. Nothing fancy, probably cost a couple of bucks from a dollar store. She reached down and flipped the face over; it was six forty-five.

Groaning at the time, she contemplated what Taryn must have felt like getting up for a five thirty shift. *Not in my lifetime.* She snaked a hand through her hair, which felt like a dustbowl had taken residence. She climbed out of bed and walked over to her bag. Unzipping the main part, she removed a toilet bag, then retrieved a towel she kept for emergencies. Some motels were not as clean as she would like, so she always carried spares. From the outside, the place looked like Taryn had described it—a dump—but the inside was clean and tidy. And from what Logan recalled of the bathroom where she'd washed up and brushed her teeth, it was very clean with a hint of bleach in the air.

Last night, she had crawled into the welcome comfort of the bed and was sound asleep before Taryn came back from the bathroom. Rude, sure, but Taryn would understand. After all, it wasn't as if they were romantically involved. *Not yet anyway.* With the way Taryn was moving on her, tonight might be a whole different ball game. With a grin, she opened the door and was a foot away from cannoning into a bear of a man who was vacating the bathroom.

"Sorry," he said, followed by words so slurred she couldn't make them out. The guy gave her the once over and then shook his head and moved down the corridor. He left with a slam of the front door. Particles of dust moved in a dance, as the sun caught them in its rays, seeping in from the window above the door.

Logan walked the couple of paces to the bathroom, and with hand on the doorknob, was about to enter when the door to the other bedroom opened. A bleary-eyed Brenda scowled at her, as the woman pulled a flimsy, scarlet dressing robe closer to her.

Not my type, lady. Logan pulled at her lower lip to prevent a smile. Then gave a tentative one. "Good morning, Mrs. Donovan."

The scowl marring the woman's face increased. "What's good about it?"

"Well, my Gran used to say it's always a good one if you wake up to take on another day."

"She was wrong." Brenda moved into the corridor, her open-toed slippers making a flip flop sound on the floorboards. "You banging my daughter?"

Logan raised her eyebrows at the crude question. *Hmm, how to answer that and not bite the hand that is currently giving me a roof over my head.* "No, what makes you say that?"

Brenda moved closer, the smell of bourbon heavy on her breath. She jabbed her finger, and although it missed the first couple of times, one artificial nail the length of a javelin made Logan wince at the pain. "The boys saw you kissing her on the porch last night. They thought it was gross. I don't want you messing with my neighbors. I've had enough trouble with the townsfolk here to last me a lifetime."

"Gross huh, I see. You obviously haven't any objection if we kiss in private where no one can see us. Is that what you're saying?" *Wow, that kid needs to leave this town.*

"I don't care what she does, as long as she doesn't bring my reputation down." Brenda shook her head and pushed Logan aside to claim the bathroom. The lock clicked behind her.

"Great, no manners. What a piece of work." Logan turned back to Taryn's bedroom and entered, leaving the door slightly ajar. She glanced at the meagre furnishings, enhanced by Taryn's own art. "All she wants is fun. Not sure how doable that is in this town, but we can try. That will be my mission for the next couple of days, to make Taryn Donovan happy in this shithole of a town."

The sound of someone being sick had Logan's stomach flipping. "Now that's what I call gross."

†

Taryn had been looking at the clock and searching the Tavern's entrance every ten minutes since she arrived for her shift. All she saw were the same tired old faces that she saw every Saturday morning. Old Mr. Timmons and his mousy wife were the first through the door, as they were every day. Taryn suspected this was their only meal of the day since it was the cheapest for the most food. They lived in a house more derelict than hers. It was seven fifteen, and a few of the hands from the Circle D drifted in. Her heart lurched. *Where is she?* Taryn didn't think Logan was a late sleeper, but what did she really know about her new friend? Just then the door swung open, and she couldn't stop the silly grin that filled her face. *Logan.*

40

"Good morning, early bird. Didn't hear you leave this morning." Logan approached Taryn with a smile.

"I didn't want to wake you." Taryn could feel a bubble of happiness fill her. "How did you sleep? That bed is so small, I'd be surprised if you were comfortable." She looked away when her face began to heat up.

"Great, it's the best night's sleep I've had since I left home." Logan moved closer and whispered, "I enjoyed the cuddling too, thank you." She kissed Taryn's cheek.

Taryn touched her cheek and blushed. "Come on, I'll show you to a booth. The special today is biscuits and gravy with hash browns, and eggs anyway you want them for five dollars. We also have the usual breakfast, if the special isn't what you want." She lifted a shoulder. "Sorry, I'm babbling. What can I get you to drink?"

"I like you babbling, so don't worry. I'll have black coffee, please, and I'll see the menu. To be honest, I'm not keen on biscuits and gravy for breakfast—more of a toast girl." Logan grinned as she sat in the booth Taryn waved her into.

Taryn handed her a menu. "Be right back with the coffee." The door opened, and six more ranch hands entered. "Crap, couldn't they have waited to come in here?" She returned to the table and poured Logan a cup of coffee. "Have you decided yet?"

"Hey, can we get some service here?" one of the ranch hands yelled.

"Be right with you." Taryn looked at Logan. "Assholes."

Logan winked. "Take your time; I'm in no rush. Serve the jerks, and then I'm sure I'll be ready to order."

"Nothing changes with them. They will order the special along with extra plates of bacon and toast. I'd rather serve you first, but if I get them out of the way I can give you all my attention…. Who am I kidding? As soon as I finish with them, more will come in. It's like a madhouse on Saturday mornings. So, have you decided yet? Probably not. Sorry. I'm so glad you're here." She put her hand to her mouth. "I'm babbling again, aren't I?"

Logan chuckled. "Yep, but it's cute. Hey, I'm a slow menu reader. I like to think on my choices. Give me five minutes and then I'll know."

"Fair enough. Take your time. You can sit there all morning if you want."

"Five minutes will be good enough for the order. I have plans to make. I'm getting lunch sorted remember?" Logan winked and picked up the menu.

An hour and a half later, Taryn sat down opposite Logan. "Finally, the rush is over. How did you like your breakfast? Sorry, all I had was time to fill your coffee cup. I'm glad you stayed. Believe it or not, it made being here tolerable for a change."

"Meal was good. It was my pleasure to stick around. Besides you might have needed a hand, and I can serve coffee for sure. So, are we still going swimming later? I'm counting on it after all the food I've just eaten." Logan picked up her coffee cup and drained the final liquid.

"You and the thought of going to my swimming hole with you kept me going all morning. Now all I need to do is make it until Vivian comes in for the lunch crowd."

"What time is that? I don't want to be late."

"Eleven. Is that okay? It's nine forty now." Taryn glanced at her watch.

"Excellent, I'll be back on the doorstep at a minute to eleven. Don't be late chatting up the locals." Logan stood and grinned.

Taryn laughed. "As if."

She watched Logan walk away and let out a long, deep sigh. The door closed only to open a moment later. Four more ranch hands walked in. She grabbed a few menus and took them over to the table they sat at. "What can I get you to drink?" After filling their coffee cups and taking their orders, she made her way over to Rosie.

"Four specials with two sides of bacon, Rosie."

"It's been a busy morning…I see your new friend came in again."

"Yeah, her car is broken, so she's stuck here until Tommy gets the parts. She's nice."

"How'd she like the lunch yesterday?"

"It was great. We ate every bit of it. She loved the chicken."

Rosie smiled. "I hear you two were kissin' on the porch last night." She eyed Taryn, "that true?"

Taryn looked at her feet. "Yeah. Those guys were giving me the business like they always do, so I gave it back to them."

"By kissin' someone…a woman…in public?"

"Sure, why not. Besides, she's a good kisser."

"Girl, you watch out. This town don't take kindly to behavior they think is different. You know that."

"I know." Taryn lifted her head and looked at Rosie. "What are they going to do to me that they haven't already?"

"Don't go givin' them more, that's all I'm sayin'"

"I know. Thanks for watching out for me, Rosie, I can always count on you." Over the years, since her grandparents died, Rosie had been there. She was more like a mother than Brenda had ever been.

"Girl, you know I care about you and don't want to see them hurt you anymore than they already have."

"I appreciate that, Rosie, probably more than you know." She reached across the counter and kissed Rosie's cheek. "Let me know when that order is up."

†

Logan couldn't recall seeing a general store but was sure there must be one, even in Bourne Falls. Walking at a fast pace, she passed a couple of closed buildings, all boarded up and in such a state of disrepair that she suspected they should really be demolished. She saw the hardware store and walked on by. *No sheriff asking after my business this time.* Two doors down, on the opposite side of the road, she saw a sign that said, *Ma Grady's Best Pies. Well, at least I've found a place, other than the tavern, that sells food.*

The building needed painting like all the rest, but the windows were clean and showed several boxes of foodstuffs. Breakfast cereal was stacked alongside a sack of wheat—animal fodder she suspected. Various other merchandise included sunglasses, hats, and newspapers. She approached and opened the yellow door. The tinkle of a bell announced her entry. Glancing around, she saw several shelves stacked with all types of tinned goods. From the far corner, a refrigerator took up the whole of the back wall.

She hadn't noticed anyone else, until a voice almost at her shoulder spoke. "What you looking for?"

Logan turned and saw a wispy beard and rotten teeth. An elderly man watched her from a few feet away.

"I'm looking for something for lunch. Do you mind if I take a look around?" She felt a bit foolish asking. *Isn't that why this is a store, so people to look around and buy?*

"Free country," he said, then began to chew on something that made a cracking sound. *Hope it isn't his teeth.*

44

Walking around the store, she selected several items and asked if she could get a box for her purchases. He gave her one reluctantly. She snagged a newspaper and paid the bill, heading out of the musty smelling place.

Hmm, that was dumb of me. What do I do with this for an hour or so until I meet up with Taryn? She frowned and pursed her lips, recalling that there was a park. At least that was the sign just as you hit the end of the main street.

A few minutes later, she was surprised to find that in such a dull town there was a small, well cared for park blooming with various flowers and bushes. The caretaker obviously had pride in his work. Standard roses in alternating colors lined the path leading to a small bandstand. "I wonder if it's still used?"

She placed her box on the floor of the stand under some shade and sat down on a seat a few feet away. She opened the newspaper and began to read the local news, not particularly about Bourne Falls but the nearest town, Sanderson Cross.

†

Logan arrived at the tavern two minutes to eleven and placed her box on the small wall dividing the path from the parking lot. The sun was shining and the day was a comfortable one in the upper seventies, certainly good enough for swimming. Although, there might be goosebumps showing up when she first hit the water. She'd spent time at the park reflecting on where her life was taking her. Taryn hadn't been wrong in suggesting that she didn't blow all her inheritance money on this trip. The more she considered Taryn's predicament, the more it reflected her own but in a different way. They both wanted the same thing—to change their lives.

45

The door to the Tavern swung open, and Taryn tripped down the few steps with a beaming smile on her face.

"Hey, you look happy. Did you have a good day at the office?" Logan grinned. Taryn's smile was rather gorgeous.

"Hey, you're here." She gave Logan a brief hug. "The morning went downhill after you left, and now it's great. Are you ready to go? No car today so we'll have to walk. Do you mind?"

"Love to walk, one of my favorite exercises." She pointed to the box on the wall. "I have lunch. Thankfully, it isn't perishable, or you'd never send me for takeout again." Logan picked up the box and turned back to Taryn. "Lead on, can't wait to get in the water today. Oh, and for the record, I'm going to win today. I even know what I'm going to wager."

"Ha, in your dreams." Taryn laughed and looked at the box. "You went to Ma Grady's? Good thing you didn't buy anything perishable…it isn't the cleanest place in town."

"Yeah, I wasn't sure if I would have to hightail it out of there and come around the tradesman's entrance to ask Rosie to help me out." Logan smiled. "I decided that you don't need to count calories, so I think I'm safe in what I got us. Right, let's go. I'm going to show you what we older women can do."

"If Rosie finds out you got something from Ma Grady and not her, I'll get into big trouble." She punched Logan in the shoulder. "You gonna show me what you older women can do, are ya? I bet you can do more than just…well swing farthest on the rope in your underwear."

"Oh, you betcha. Come on, you wench, it's time to show me how conciliatory you can be in defeat."

Twenty minutes later, Logan placed the box on the stone they had rested on the night before and flexed her shoulder muscles. Taryn had asked often if she wanted to share the load, but that wouldn't have been right. Any butch worth their salt would have called her a wuss. Taryn instead had talked knowledgeably about world and local affairs— definitely not a hick-town girl. The town and its people suppressed her, but if the woman could just get out there and see what life had to offer, she would be a star. *Yeah and where is that coming from? You hardly know her*. The voice inside her head that had helped her manage her breakup spoke for the first time in years.

Taryn grinned and began pulling off her uniform. "If you think you have any chance of beating me, you're gonna have to get rid of those clothes."

Logan pulled herself out of her musings and laughed. "Remember we older ones can be wiser, and who said anything about clothes being a barrier? Logan stuck out her tongue and jumped into the cold water. "Damn that's freezing." She shook her head like a dog and waved at Taryn who was still on the rock.

"Freezing? What a wuss you are." Taryn jumped into the water, splashing it in all directions. "Catch me if you can," she said before swimming away.

Logan watched Taryn frolicking in the water for a few seconds, realizing that it made her feel ten years younger. That was something she wanted, no needed, and perhaps was looking for on this journey. Not the younger part exactly, but being alive and wanting another person's company. "Told you we older ones have tricks up our sleeves." She swam toward Taryn and reached out to take her arm.

Taryn swung around and pulled Logan to her. "Care to show me those tricks?" She kissed her cheek and pulled away laughing.

Logan held onto Taryn and tugged her unresisting body closer. "I told you we older ones have tricks." Her lips captured Taryn's and explored them slowly, waiting for her to pull away. She didn't. Logan probed for more, running her tongue along Taryn's lips before they opened and their tongues entwined.

Taryn melted into Logan. Ever since she first saw her, she'd longed to feel the taut body next to hers. She couldn't remember ever feeling as happy as she did since meeting Logan. For her, it was like dancing on the wind while floating high above the town of Bourne Falls, with all the residents looking up at her with envy. She knew that Logan wanted her, and she took her tongue fully into her mouth and reveled in the sensation. When they finally pulled apart, she said, "God, that's the first time anyone has kissed me. It's fantastic."

"Well, I have to say, Miss Novice, you are a great kisser." Logan recaptured her lips.

This time, the exploration took a whole different dimension, and Taryn closed her eyes, delighting in the sensations coursing through her body. The feel of Logan's breasts against hers was like nothing she'd ever experienced. All she knew was that she wanted to know the woman in her arms on every level imaginable and maybe even some no one had ever thought of. She pulled back and looked directly into the green eyes that were so close to her. "Teach me." She swallowed hard. "Show me how to love you," she whispered.

"Too soon, I want your first to be with someone you love or at least care for a lot. I can't take your virginity, Taryn. It wouldn't be right."

Taryn pulled away. "No problem. I'm sorry. We should go and eat now." She gave Logan a slight nod and swam toward the rock.

Seconds later, Logan caught her arm. "Okay, so you're pissed and I understand that, but I'm thinking about what's good for you and ultimately me. Do you know how easy it is for me to fall for you? I'm gone in a few days. I won't do that, Taryn, not to you or any other woman, and especially not to me. What I do know is that if it's meant to be it will be."

Taryn's head moved upward. "Another quote from your gran I suppose."

"Yes, it is. You are so refreshing in my life, Taryn, and I want to get it right. Care to have lunch with me…after the wager?"

The words made sense, but Taryn was finding it hard to look at Logan. After the high she'd felt, she was now free falling. *Stupid, stupid, stupid.* "Sure, let's go."

"Okay, I'm first, age before beauty." Logan swam toward the rope swing.

Taryn watched Logan swim away then swam after her. *If this is my brass ring, I'm gonna try and hold on for as long as I can.*

CHAPTER FIVE

Taryn flew into the Tavern to find Vivian tapping her toe. "You're late."

"I'm sorry, I lost track of time."

"I was supposed to get my kids twenty-five minutes ago. Now I have to pay the sitter more." Vivian slapped a check at Taryn's chest. "This is the check for table twelve. Make sure I get my tip." She let out a harrumph and walked away.

The only thing Taryn could do was smile. Even though she had completely embarrassed herself by wanting to make love with Logan, she'd had a fantastic afternoon. After the rope challenge that Logan won, they ate the surprisingly good lunch. The rest of the time they'd lain on the rock talking, laughing, and drying off.

Taryn had been in the shadows, but now, with Logan, she was a someone who mattered. That was exhilarating. Nothing that Vivian or anyone else said to her could ruin her day. The dinner crowd began to drift in, and she smiled knowing Logan would arrive later. A tingle ran through her body in anticipation.

†

Logan knocked on the peeling, worn-paint door, not sure what to expect. The morning's encounter with Brenda hadn't gone well, and she hoped the woman wasn't home. At the same time, Logan needed to get inside and change her clothes.

The door thrust open. "You. What is it now? Taryn is working."

About what I expected. "I need a change of clothes. I promised your daughter to be at the tavern tonight." Logan shrugged. "I also wondered if there was anything I could help out with for you allowing me to stay here."

"Hmm, you should be grateful and groveling at my feet. She's like her dad, too damn soft and always tinkering with stuff when he wasn't working. A fucking waste of time if you ask me."

Circumstances often had a lot to do with perception of life, and Logan had held a kernel of hope that Taryn's mother maybe wasn't that bad. *Guess not.* "So," she tried again, "is there anything you want done? I'm at a loose end for a few hours."

"Take your pick. Everything needs repairing. Taryn is too busy in her own world to do anything around here."

Logan took a chance and placed a hand on Brenda's arm. It was immediately shrugged off. *So be it.* "Any objection if I fix the squeaky floorboards on the porch and—" she saw Brenda scowl. "I'll just do my thing."

She watched Brenda traverse several expressions until her face morphed into a sneer. "Do what you want. I have some friends coming this afternoon, and I don't want you in the way." Brenda stalked off but left the door open.

Logan grinned. *Gran, you were right. Little steps to reach the goal, but this is a hard road to travel.*

†

Taryn glanced at the door for the hundredth time in the last hour. The Tavern was noisier than she'd ever heard, with every loud talker for miles around there at the same time. Usually, that kind of thing didn't bother her, because she had become adept at filtering everything out. Today, it seemed deafening. Even with all the people and noise surrounding her, she was alone. With Logan, she wasn't alone, and she couldn't wait to see her.

The door swung open, and she almost dropped the tray of meatloaf specials trying to see who it was. *Damn. Just another one of the regulars.* She served a table of five and moved back toward the counter where Rosie had placed another order.

"Think this will die down soon?" Taryn put two plates on her tray.

"You don't usually work Saturday nights, Taryn. They are always a ruckus, and this place doesn't shut down until late." Rosie laughed and shook her head. "They do like Karaoke night. Next order will be up when you come back."

Taryn sighed and lifted the tray. *Where can she be?* Just as she served the plates to a table near the door, it opened. When she looked up, the sight took her breath away. Logan coming in the door was a vision in a sea of the mundane. Her white-blonde hair was pulled back so tightly, all that was visible was her face. She wore a form-fitting, white shirt with a narrow, black tie running down its length to black leather pants and knee-high, black boots. She was, in one word—hot. The tight-fitting shirt and pants accentuated every curve of her body. A body that Taryn was intimately

52

acquainted with. She noticed the noise level in the room had died down. All the men and many of the woman were slack jawed as they stared at Logan.

Taryn swallowed hard and moved toward her friend. "Hey, you made it." *Breathe.* "I've been watching that door all night, waiting for you to come through it." *Stay cool.* "Let me show you to a table." Her eyes took in the rest of the people and smiled. *I've seen her almost naked.* "Come on, I've been saving a table for you."

Logan placed a hand on Taryn's arm. "You're babbling again, I'm going to be here until you finish your shift, so don't panic that I'll run out on you." Logan chuckled. "Do you like the outfit? Think it's different enough to be noticed?"

"Oh, no worries on that front. Did you see all the men—and women—with their tongues hanging out when you came in?"

"Nope, they don't interest me. I dressed to impress one person and one person only."

Taryn smiled. "And who would that be?"

"Well the prettiest girl in this place, for sure, and she's standing right next to me. Are you happy with that?" Logan winked and took the seat at the table Taryn indicated.

"Happy? Didn't you see my tongue hanging down to the floor? You are h-o-t...hot."

Logan laughed. "Good to know. Now, I'm sure you need to work and not talk to me all night. Not that I wouldn't want that. Anything you recommend on the specials list tonight? I'm famished."

Rosie was ringing the pick-up bell incessantly. "Duty calls. Fried chicken is the special tonight, although the chicken-fried steak is good too." The bell rang again. "Darn, she's persistent." Taryn shot Logan an apologetic glance.

"Go for it. As you know, I like to take my time over the menu."

Taryn walked quickly to the window. "Okay, I'm here now."

"You got work to do, so stop hanging around that hottie." Rosie grinned and shook her head. "Let me know what she wants, and I'll give her an extra portion."

Taryn loaded plates on her tray and delivered the meals to a table by the bar before swinging by the other tables to see if they needed anything. Finished for the moment, she hurried back to Logan's table. "You decided yet?"

"Absolutely, ma'am. Chicken-fried steak and instead of fries, any chance of hash browns? I love hash browns. A weakness of mine." Logan flipped the menu over and handed it to Taryn. "I'll have whatever beer is on tap."

"Good choice. I'm not sure about the hash browns, but I bet Rosie can get them for you." Taryn began to leave then turned around. "You are, by far, the best looking, hottest woman in the place."

"Then I made good choices. When do you have a break?"

Taryn looked at her watch. "In about half an hour. Let me put your order in and make sure everyone has what they need." She made her way to Rosie and handed her the order. "Can she have hash browns instead of fries with that?

"Sure thing."

Taryn turned to leave and heard Rosie say, "I'm glad you've found a friend."

"Me too," Taryn said over her shoulder with a big smile. "Me too."

Logan watched Taryn leave the table, and her gaze fixed on the pert bottom that swung gently with every step.

How the hell did the people around here miss that? Their loss and my gain. And what a gain. A deep voice, well within ear shot, rang out.

"Do you see that dyke? She's giving Taryn an education. When she's done with her and leaves town, I'm going to see what the girl has been taught."

The hair on the back of Logan's neck stood up. Exactly what she was afraid of for Taryn. The kid was too innocent to know this kind of thing happened. She moved her feet around under the table and clenched her fists, as the companions of the loud mouth roared in laughter and gave wolf whistles. *Do I deck them now or later? Hmm, I need the food fix first, but they are most definitely on my hit list for later.* She switched her gaze to the table, and all eyes from the three scruffy-looking men focused on her.

"Oops, nearly forgot your beer, and Rosie can do the hash browns just for you." The mug was placed on the table, and Taryn left as quickly as she arrived.

Logan smirked at the men and lifted the beer to her mouth, drank down a large mouthful, and smacked her lips. Her eyes never left the bulging eyes of the men who found her and Taryn entertaining. The rest of the crowd was mainly male with a scattering of women. Most of the people appeared to be as she suspected, middle aged, although some were around Taryn's age. *Probably from that ranch Taryn spoke about.*

A large poster on the door indicated that it was karaoke night. *That sort of thing always brings the crowds out.* With a slight smile, she turned her attention back to Taryn who was a few tables away serving drinks. Their eyes met and she winked, noticing that the men's eyes were still glued to her. She picked up her glass. Before taking a drink, she wet her lips with an exaggerated move of her tongue. Their expressions immediately fixated on her mouth. She mouthed, *no way*, before drinking more of her beer.

Taryn came back with Logan's order and placed the plate in front of her before taking the seat next to her. "I've got a few minutes. The dinner crowd is thinning out, and now it's time for the drinkers and drunks." She grinned. "Leaning heavily toward the drunks."

Logan nodded. "I know. That table over to the left is pretty loud, and a couple of them look familiar. Will you thank Rosie for me? Hash browns really are my favorite."

Taryn looked in the direction of the table of men. "I like to call them the three stooges. They have no jobs, so they spend their days and nights here before they go home and beat on the little woman." She blew out a breath. "God, I hate this town. I'll let Rosie know. Can I get you anything else?"

"Ah, that's why they look familiar. I saw them propping up the bar yesterday. Another beer will be good."

"You got it. I should be on my break when you've finished your meal, which works out perfectly. I'll have that beer sent over."

"Thank you for taking care of me. You are doing a superb job."

"It's easy to do for you. I should be the one thanking you." She got up. "See you in a few."

"Look forward to it."

Taryn smiled as she sashayed away. Logan's eyes never left Taryn's body, watching the movement something she would never get tired of seeing. Picking up the knife and fork, she looked down at the delicious-smelling food and began to eat her meal.

Five minutes later, a beer was slapped on the table and surprisingly it didn't spill. Logan looked up into the blue eyes of a pretty woman. By the few lines around her eyes,

Logan deduced she was in her thirties. "Why thank you, ma'am." She smiled.

The woman seemed flustered at her politeness and stared at her.

"Anything wrong, Miss…?"

"Oh, well no, not really. You're that lesbeen friend of Taryn's, ain't ya?"

Logan scratched the side of her neck. *Interesting pronunciation.* "Yep, I sure am, ma'am. It's good to meet you, I'm Logan." She held out her hand and stopped herself from giggling as the woman hesitated to take it. She eventually did.

"Mary Dixon, I'm the bar help on a Saturday, being Karaoke night and all. I can get you the list, if you're interested. We could do with some new blood around here."

Logan held onto the hand a little longer than normal and saw the woman blush—it matched her outfit. "I love those boots, true cowgirl with the light tan and pink, and all those super flowers. Did you get them around here?"

"Hell, no. In this town? You gotta be joking. Ordered them from a place in Texas. Thank God for the internet. So, are you interested?"

Logan shrugged. "Let me ask my friend when she comes back, and I'll let you know."

The woman looked in Taryn's direction. "Probably no then. She doesn't mix with anyone in town. Then you have her mother, who mixes with every one of the male gender. Wave at me when you need a refill."

Logan nodded and shook her head before going back to demolishing her meal. *Interesting town.*

Taryn stood with clenched fists, as Mary Dixon, of all people, seemed to be coming on to Logan. "That bitch. Logan is my friend, not hers."

"Something botherin' you?" Rosie asked.

"No. Why would it?" Taryn could hear the edge to her voice and tried to breathe through her anger. It didn't work.

"Well you're standing there stiff as a board, glaring at poor Mary who ain't got the brain God gave her. I think she was dropped as a baby."

"I think she's trying to make a move on my friend. That's what I think."

"Whatcha going to do about it?"

"Punch her lights out."

Rosie had a surprised look on her face. "Taryn Donovan, I can't believe you said that. I've never thought you were violent."

"I'm not, Rosie. I just don't like her making a move on my friend."

"It's your break time. Why not get over there and claim her?"

"I think I will."

Taryn walked quickly to Logan's table. "I'm on break now. Do you want to come outside with me?"

"Can I finish my meal first? Almost done, only need a couple more minutes. I don't want to waste the hash browns." Logan frowned. "Anything wrong?"

Taryn plopped down on a chair. "Sorry, I didn't notice. To be honest, I saw you talking to Mary, and it looked really friendly." She eyed Logan. "You know she was dropped as a baby...at least that's what Rosie told me." Taryn could feel her face heat up. "That was an ugly thing to say. I don't know what's wrong with me. Oh no, I'm rambling again, aren't I?"

Logan placed her cutlery down and stared at Taryn. "Outside, now." She stood.

Taryn cringed, but got up and followed Logan outside. Wolf whistles, catcalls, and lewd noises followed them out the door.

†

Outside, Taryn placed her arms over her breast defensively, much as she did when her mother berated her. "What?"

"What, you ask *me* what. How old are you?"

Confused, Taryn took a step back. "I'm twenty-four." Why?

"You are not acting like it. For the record, I'm thirty-two and as I've told you, I've been around the block. One thing I don't do is play with people or degrade them in someone else's eyes unless it's the truth. Are you a woman or a child?"

Ashamed, Taryn looked away. "I've never had a friend, and I thought maybe you were…I guess I just blew it." She shrugged and turned to walk away.

"It was a simple question, Taryn, and all you do is walk away."

With tears brimming in her eyes, Taryn turned back to Logan. "Life has taught me that the best choice is to walk away. That way no one can hurt me. I'm sorry."

"You think I will hurt you? Have I done anything, so far, that has hurt you? I don't need sorry, Taryn, it doesn't work for me."

Even though she told herself she didn't care about what others said about her, the sting had always hurt. In that moment, the frustration built up all through her life exploded, and she began to pound Logan's chest before collapsing in tears. "You are the only person I've ever let in," she sobbed.

Logan touched Taryn's shoulder. "So, tell me, are you a woman or a child?"

Taryn snorted. "After my father died, Brenda never let me be a child. For as long as I can remember, I've had to be the adult." She chewed on her lip. "I'm a woman."

"Good, because what I'm about to do now, I'd never do to a child." Logan reached out and pulled Taryn into her arms and kissed her.

Taryn melted into the lips that touched hers, and she felt her body soar. When they broke apart, she looked at Logan. "You like me, you really like me."

"Oh, trust me, I like you. Do you know how hard it was for me not to take you at the swimming hole?" Logan touched her forehead to Taryn's.

"Can we kiss some more? I've never been kissed until you came into my life, and now I don't want to stop."

Logan pulled away and smiled, then touched Taryn's nose. "For the new woman in my life, you got it." Then they locked lips again.

In the background, Taryn heard some drunk butchering the words to "Moon River," and she pulled away. "God, they're starting already. It's going to be a long night."

Logan laughed. "Oh, I don't know, I think prospects are looking up." Logan snatched a swift kiss. "Let's go back inside, I don't want you in any trouble with your employer for overstaying your break."

Taryn kissed Logan then took her hand. "For you, it would be worth it. Come on, let's go see how many catcalls we can get this time."

"Works for me."

†

Taryn was holding Logan's hand when they entered the Tavern. She knew there would be crude remarks, but she didn't really care. *Let them think what they want. I'm happy for the first time in forever, and I'm going to keep that feeling for as long as I can.*

She turned to Logan. "I've got another two hours before my shift is over." She could feel a tightening in her chest. Not being with Logan and able to touch her for that long seemed like an eternity. She led Logan to a booth. "Take a seat, and I'll get you something to drink. Is beer okay?"

"Sounds good to me."

Taryn shivered when Logan winked at her. "Be right back."

The hour dragged on for Taryn, most of her time devoted to delivering drinks to men drunk or on their way there. She had to keep on her toes to avoid the hands that were always aiming at her backside or her breasts. So that she'd have an excuse to stop at Logan's table, she made sure that she kept her beer mug refreshed.

"Just thirty minutes to go and we can get out of here." Taryn set a bowl of peanuts on the table. "Can I get you anything else?" She frowned when the woman singing "Delta Dawn" was so off key it hurt her ears. "I could do better than that, and I don't sing." She laughed. "She'll probably win the prize, as the judges are all dirty old men and she has big jugs." Taryn shrugged. "That's how it usually works around here."

"Big jugs huh, works for me too." Logan grinned.

"Oh, you." Taryn slapped Logan's arm. "You ready for another or have you reached your limit?"

"No limit for me, darlin'. I think I'm gonna stand at the bar. That way you don't have to waste your energy waiting on me." Logan stood.

Taryn grinned. "I can't think of anyone else I'd rather wait on. Go stand by the bar, and then I can see you each time I get drinks." She winked at Logan. "You gonna sing tonight? The prize is a hundred dollars."

"Really? A hundred bucks…hmm, let me think on it. Now go, wench, and finish your shift so we can have fun." Logan winked.

With a hearty laugh and a kiss to Logan's cheek, Taryn walked away dreaming of the fun they would have later that night. She was oblivious of the men watching her.

Logan walked over to the bar, surprised at how steady she was. Normally, drinking three beers was enough for her. She'd had five now, and was about to sink at least another before Taryn's shift finished. She slid onto the only free seat, separating a couple of guys who appeared to be close to falling off their wooden stools. She suspected that only clutching their bottles kept them upright.

"What can I get you?' A surly voice asked.

Logan stared at the bartender, a wiry guy with a full beard and piglet eyes. He wasn't handsome in any way, shape, or form, but she wasn't any sort of judge. No man was attractive to her.

"Beer, not sure of the name."

"Hey, you decided to come visit instead of keeping yourself holed up in that corner. Gonna have a go on the stage? We have openings in half an hour." Mary pointed to the beer on tap. "She's having that one."

With a grunt, the beer was drawn and banged down in front of her, the froth tipping over onto the counter. Logan nodded at the man before smiling at Mary.

"Might do that. Did you say there's a list of songs?"

"Oh, there sure is. Let me get it for you." Mary dropped down behind the counter. She reappeared seconds later, waving a ragged looking sheaf of papers in her hand. "Here you go."

Logan took the pages and smiled at Mary again. "Thanks, I'll let you know."

Sipping her beer, Logan began looking at the list. Old songs from the '60s, '70s, and '80s filled most of the sheets. *Damn, I'm not old enough to remember some of these.*

"I think you should sing 'Stand by your Man.'"

Logan turned to the man on her left. "Really, you do huh? What makes you think I'd be interested in that song?"

Bleary, partially bloodshot, grey eyes gazed at her. Logan looked at his pasty face and lips that seemed to droop as if he'd had a stroke.

"You're a woman, so why not? All the ladies around here sing that song."

"Oh." Logan ran her tongue around the inside of her mouth, trying to stifle the laughter. "I'm not from around here, and I have a different view of what I'd sing."

The man looked her up and down. "Yeah, you sure are different. You dress like a man. What do you do for a living? Can't say I've seen the likes of you in this place before, and I've lived here forty years."

Logan smiled, sipped her beer, and nodded. "I work in an office in Chicago, so you wouldn't have seen *the likes of me* around town. Do you sing?"

The man laughed. "Only in the bathroom. I do a mean 'King of the Road' though, if I say so myself." He picked up his empty bottle and tried to drink from it.

63

"Yeah, I do a mean song in the bathroom too. I'm Logan." She held out her hand, and the man shook it weakly.

"Davy, I'm the bank teller in town. So, what you gonna sing?"

Logan was about to reply when Taryn tapped her on the shoulder.

"Are you okay? He isn't bothering you, is he?"

"Go on and git. I'm talking to the lady," Davy said.

Logan bristled. "Hey, that's no way to talk to a lady, Davy, especially this lady…. She's mine."

"She's yours?" Davy laughed. "Whatcha wanna do with her when you can have me, little lady."

Taryn shook her head and picked up a tray of drinks. "Catch you later, *little lady*." She laughed and walked away.

"Ah, Davy, you don't have the curves in the right places or the equipment, if you get my drift." Logan winked, thankful there wasn't a scene. She could cope with one but didn't want to have Taryn suffer the fall out when she left town.

Davy frowned, obviously struggling with the concept.

"I prefer a woman in my arms than a man. Is that a problem for you?" Logan stared at the man, and he scratched one of his straw-colored eyebrows.

"Naw, she's got steel knickers, and no one has ever got to first base with her, from what I hear. Her mother on the other hand—"

Logan raised her hand. "How about I buy you another beer, and you can help me select a song. Sound good to you?"

Davy's face beamed. "Lady, I hope you get lucky tonight."

Logan rolled her eyes and waved over Mary to serve them more beer. *Oh, I know that can happen. The thing is, would that be the right thing to do?*

64

"Gotta take a leak," Davy said before walking away on unsteady legs and feet.

Logan struggled to focus on her watch. Taryn was due soon. *Crap, I'm drunk. She's going to think I'm like the rest of them around here. Water is good, really good they say.*

"Here you go, Logan, Davy put this in for you." The beer sloshed as it landed on the counter.

"Great, thanks. Is he coming back?" She creased her brow.

"Yes. Oh, he's a banker, and they have a routine. He won't be staying much longer."

"But tomorrow is Sunday and not a banking day."

Mary shrugged. "His kids are in Brighton, and he does a Skype chat with them every Sunday. He never misses. Good guy. Really a pity that his wife died," Mary said as she began to wash glasses.

Logan sighed heavily. "That's sad, Mary, why doesn't he have the kids?"

Mary rolled her eyes and continued her task of washing glasses. Logan wasn't sure she was going to get an answer. It surprised her when she did.

"The wife's parents thought he wasn't good enough for their only child, and he went off the rails when she died. They took advantage and got custody of the kids. He's just another sad sack in this town."

Logan was about to respond, when Mary left to take care of another customer. *Wow, this town is unlucky.* She sighed and turned her attention to the rest of the room, knowing that the only bright spot would be Taryn, who didn't think she was worth a second look. *How wrong she is.*

"Hey, I've finished."

Logan looked into the innocent eyes of the young woman who had done something no one else had in her lifetime—given Logan everything she dreamed of without any ties.

"Great, I missed you. Wanna sing 'Flashdance' with me? I'm up in ten minutes. We can sing something else though…Davy wasn't that good with the songs."

Taryn shook her head. "'Flashdance' is not a good choice. How about 'Somebody to Love?'"

Logan began humming the song. "Good one and very fitting for you."

"Are you sure you're up for singing tonight?" Logan was slurring slightly, and her eyes were dilated. She looked cute.

Just then, there was an uproar, and most of the men began chanting "Brenda, Brenda."

"Damn, that's all I need." It wasn't a minute before Brenda was grabbing hold of her arm and pulling her away from Logan and the bar.

"How dare you flaunt your affair with that woman all over town."

"You're up, blondie." Taryn heard Fred call.

"I don't have time for you right now, Brenda." Taryn turned away and smiled at Logan. "Come on. Let's see if we can win the money." She took Logan's hand and led her to the small area where the karaoke machine was. "We're going to sing *Somebody to Love*, Fred."

"Okay, let me cue it up."

Logan began by playing an air piano, and Taryn strutted around the small stage as best she could. She brought the mic to her mouth and began singing the words she saw on the screen. All the while, Logan was next to her, singing. She moved closer to Taryn, playing an air guitar, and kissed Taryn's cheek while she sang. The room went in a free-for-all, as the crowd got up and sang along. The voices were deafening. "…somebody, somebody…" Taryn belted out a few more lines before bumping hips with Logan so that they were gyrating against one another. She stopped and looked out at all the people watching…and sang. "Somebody…to love."

Vaguely, in the background, Taryn could hear cat whistles and appreciative applause. None of that mattered—only Logan mattered, her hot breath seemed to be all over Taryn's body. Logan played one more air-guitar riff, and Taryn sang "somebody…" once more, and the song ended.

As she was walking back to the bar, Taryn expected Brenda to berate her. No worries there, Brenda was near the door, making out with one of her regular boyfriends.

"Hey, that was a blast. Shall we do another?" Logan slurred.

Taryn grabbed on Logan's arm and pulled her in for a kiss. "No more songs. Let's go home."

"Well, that's an invitation I'm not going to pass. Let me say bye to Davy. I think he was clapping the loudest, and we did get the crowd going." Logan settled her head on Taryn's shoulder. "You are one mean singer, Taryn. I'm finding out you're a woman with many talents."

"Talents maybe, but I am always willing to learn. I think you are probably a very good teacher." She bumped Logan with her hip and pointed down the bar. "Davy is over there. You know that most of the people here would say you're wasting your time on him."

"I can tell he's a good guy underneath all the drink. Sometimes life takes pot shots at us, big time. We either surrender and go under, or we fight and kick ass. I'm the kick ass type of girl with my life. What about you?" Logan kissed the side of Taryn's neck.

"Davy is one of the decent ones but…" Taryn shook her head. "I get the feeling that the people in this town look down on people like Davy and me like we're some sort of trash, and we're not…just different."

Logan shifted to look directly into Taryn's eyes and placed her hands on her shoulders. "Give them a chance to get to know you, Taryn." Taryn pursed her lips, and Logan traced a finger over them. "If you live in the past, darling, the past controls you. I know you can break free of that. In fact, you already have. You are here with me, knowing that your mother doesn't approve."

Taryn snorted. "She doesn't care what I do, as long as she can bring the men home with her and I stay out of the way." She looked at Brenda kissing a scruffy looking ranch hand and laughed. "She has no taste but…." She ran a finger down the middle of Logan's chest. "I don't take after her." She grinned. "I have great taste."

Just at that moment, Roger Murdock and his wife Rachel approached them. "Taryn, I never knew you had such a wonderful voice," Rachel said. "Our church choir is always looking for people to join us."

Taryn could feel her cheeks heat. "Um, thank you. I'll think about it." She watched the couple go and turned to Logan. "I didn't think they knew my name."

Logan chuckled. "Hey, it's amazing what people know but don't actually say. Who are they?"

"He's a builder. They come in here every Friday for dinner." Taryn shrugged. "I've never heard them call me by name before." She smiled at Logan. "I think you are improving my reputation."

Logan pulled Taryn close. "Anything to oblige, my lady." She bowed and almost fell over.

"Logan, I do believe you are drunk. What do you say I take you home and put you to bed?"

Logan grinned. "I don't usually drink this much. Three is my limit. Can I say bye to Davy? I like him."

Taryn took her hand. "Come on, I'll keep you upright while you talk to Davy." She led Logan through the crowd to Davy, who was sitting at the far end of the bar. "Mr. Randal, Logan wants to speak to you."

"Hey, my strange friend, that was great up there on the stage. Are you going to do it next week?"

"I'm out of here on Tuesday. I'm going back home to Chicago. It was a pleasure to meet you, Davy. I hope you get your kids back real soon." Logan took Davy's hand and shook it hard and began to move away.

Suddenly, the realization of what Logan said hit Taryn in the gut, hard. *Has this all been a dream? She'll be gone, and I'll be back to the same old same old I've been doing all my life.* She tugged on Logan's sleeve. "Are you really leaving so soon? I just got to know you."

"My life isn't in Bourne Falls, Taryn. You know that. Remember, I'm only here because my car broke down."

Taryn knew better but blurted out, "I should have known better. I trusted you and thought you were my friend." She ignored the startled look on Logan's face and continued. "What am I, Logan, some hick girl from Bumfuck, Nowhere who amused you because you had nothing better to do?" Taryn looked away instantly knowing she'd crossed a line she might never be able to go back to. *Oh god, what have I done?*

Logan lifted her hands in the air and frowned. "Okay, I've had a drink and you haven't, so technically, we might be on different planes here. But that was so totally out of order. I'm not surprised you don't have any friends here if this is how you act. You have a mercurial temperament, for sure." Logan turned to Davy. "Next drink is on me. Taryn, you can join us or not. Your call. I'm having another beer with

69

someone who isn't judging me." She called over the bartender and ordered two drinks.

"Can I talk to you before you and Davy have that drink? Please?"

Logan shook her head. "Nope, you made your call. I'm making mine. What are you having? Or is drinking with Davy and me too low for you to go?"

Taryn wiped a tear from her eye. "Look, my mother is the town whore. I live in a rundown shack. I have a dead-end job, and the only joy I've ever known is when I work with designing things out of metal. Until…you walked in that door. My world has changed because of you, Logan." She looked away then back directly in Logan's eyes. "I'm sorry for what I said. Just know I'll never be sorry for meeting you." A smile creased her lips. "I will be forever grateful for knowing you." With a lift of one shoulder, she turned and walked away.

CHAPTER SIX

Taryn, with her shoulders and back straight, walked out the Tavern's door into the warm night air. She swiped hot tears off her cheeks. She kept half expecting to hear Logan's voice but knew she wouldn't. *What was I thinking? She'll leave in a few days, and I always knew that.* Life had taught her not to expect anything from anyone, but somehow, she'd forgotten that lesson where it concerned Logan. She fisted her hands at her side. *I bet she finds someone to toy with in every town she goes to.* She smacked her head. *What a fool I was. If the town wasn't laughing at me before, they are now.*

She trudged resolutely down the street to the rundown place she called home. She would take Logan's belongings and place them outside and lock the door.

You're being childish, her inner voice said.

"I know, but the only way I know to stop the pain is to remove her from my life."

Is that what you want to do? the voice countered.

"Nooo. I want her in my life."

Taryn stepped up on the porch. When she automatically extended her step over the broken floorboard, she stopped and looked around. Someone had fixed the floorboards, and the screen door no longer listed to one side. *There is no way one of Brenda's boyfriends would do something like this—all they want to do is fuck her and nothing more.*

"Logan." The realization of who had done the repairs shook Taryn to her heart. She tried to remember when anyone had done anything for Brenda out of the generosity of their heart. "Yet, Logan has, and I was awful to her." She turned, ready to run back to the Tavern and ask Logan to forgive her. She'd known from the start how temporary the situation was. The realization of that hit her. Logan would leave, thinking of her as nothing more than a childish crybaby.

"Logan showed me that I'm better than that." With her stomach churning, she ran as fast as she could back to the Tavern and Logan. There was no way she'd squander the opportunity that Logan offered her. If she had to, she'd fall to her knees and beg.

When she pushed open the Tavern's door, Mary Peabody, the fifth-grade teacher, was at the microphone blathering on about a song she wanted to sing. Taryn's eyes went at once to the bar. The woman who made her heart sing was sitting there. Her feet moved as though they were floating on air, until she stopped behind Logan.

†

Logan felt the hairs on the back of her neck rise, as a breath fanned her skin. She slowly smiled around the neck of the beer bottle she was drinking from. "I ordered you a beer and coke, not together of course."

"You knew I'd be back."

Logan placed the bottle on the counter and spun around, her legs touching the top of Taryn's thighs.

Logan wagged a finger, then smiled. "I never take things for granted, but I hoped you would. You're a woman right, not a child?"

Taryn shook her head slowly and smiled. "Yes, I'm a woman. One day, I hope you find out just how much," she whispered.

Logan felt wetness flooding her center at that comment. She'd seen this woman almost naked, and it was an amazing sight. She motioned to the seat next to her. In the background, Mary was murdering *Stand by your Man*. "Can't vouch for the singing, but it would be a pleasure to have your company. I missed you."

Taryn sat and then looked around. "Where's Davy?"

"He went home, and took the beer with him. He said his priority was to be, at least, awake for the Skype call from his kids in the morning." Logan shrugged and sipped more of her beer.

"Thank you."

"For what?"

Taryn stared at Logan. "Maybe I shouldn't be thanking you but Shelia. After all, if it hadn't been for her meltdown, you wouldn't have stopped. Would you?"

Logan frowned. "True, this is the first place I've actually interacted with locals in two months of travelling. I was ready to go home and buy a cat for company." She chuckled.

"I'm glad Shelia decided to take a break here. Thank you for showing me that not everyone around this town thinks I'm...well, you know...not worthy." Taryn sipped her beer.

Logan watched her drink and then took her hand. "Thank you for allowing me to know what living is all about again. I'm a big believer in the idea that things happen for a reason. Our meeting was good for both of us, don't you think?"

"Oh, yes, I do. You know, when I left earlier, it was mostly because I was suddenly unnerved by you."

"By me?"

"Yes. I let mediocrity rule my life for so long that I let myself believe that was all I deserved. Until you came along. It was easy to let the excuse of being Brenda's daughter shape my life." She shrugged. "I didn't need to take chances and try to make friends with her as an excuse for everything that is wrong in my life." Taryn took a swig of her beer. "But it isn't my mother's fault. I never demanded anything better, because I didn't think I was worth it…but I am." She took Logan's hand. "I want to make the most of the time we have before Shelia is fixed and you have to go."

"And, you're okay with that?"

"Yes. Yes, I am. Some time with you is better than no time at all."

Logan grinned. "Well I guess then, that the next two days are going to be a blast." She yawned. "Guess I've had more than my limit. I'm beat. Shall we head off home now?"

Taryn took Logan's hand. "I think there's a warm bed waiting for us. Come on, let's go."

†

It was quiet when they arrived back at the house. Taryn turned to Logan and hugged her. "Thank you for doing all this work to the porch. It makes the house look a hundred percent better. What did Brenda say about it?"

"She was silent on the matter, although I'm pretty sure I saw a smile."

"Brenda is not the warm and cuddly type." Taryn looked at Logan and wiggled her eyebrows. "Are you?"

Logan chuckled, then placed a finger to her lips. "Don't tell anyone, but I've been told I give great bear hugs."

Taryn opened the door and listened. There were no sounds, and she let out a breath before closing her eyes sending up a small prayer that Brenda wouldn't be home any time soon. "Come on in. Can I get you something to drink or eat?" She cocked her head to one side. "Drink is something I can promise we have, as for food…well, unless I bring it home from the Tavern, there won't be much here."

Logan shook her head. "I think I was drinking the tavern dry. As for food, I haven't eaten so well in years. I'm going to get fat." She stumbled as she followed Taryn through the door.

"Fat? You, never." Taryn took Logan's hand again and led her to the bedroom. "Come on, let's get you undressed and ready for bed. You look like you're going to fall over."

"Oooh, now that's an offer I'm not refusing…a beautiful woman undressing me."

Taryn gulped back the fear she was feeling. She'd seen Logan in only her underwear and bra, while they were swimming, but now she was dressed and wanting Taryn to undress her. This was far more intimate than swimming. With nervous fingers, she reached to loosen the tie, then unbuttoned the shirt Logan was wearing and lowered it down her arms. She wasn't wearing a bra. Taryn sucked in a breath when she saw the creamy white breasts punctuated with brown nipples. The sight took her breath away, and she could feel stirrings she'd never experienced before. "Is this okay?" She shrugged. "I've never done this before."

"Whoa, I really like this experience, but it's making me dizzy. I think I'm going to fall over." Logan collapsed on the bed, her arms flat on the cover and her feet in the air. She began to quietly snore.

Taryn just shook her head. "My big chance to be with a woman and she faints on me." She took off her boots and undid the belt buckle before unzipping Logan's leather pants and pulling them down her legs. Next, she pulled Logan up the bed, rolled her to the side, and slid the sheet and blanket down. It took some effort, but she was finally able to get Logan under the covers. Taryn kissed her lips gently and smiled. "You are something else, Logan Perry." With a wistful sigh, Taryn undressed and crawled in next to Logan, draping an arm over her.

Logan snuggled closer to Taryn and slurred, "Nice, I could get used to this."

Taryn smiled at the comment. "I could too," she said before joining Logan in sleep.

†

Logan slowly lifted her head. The smell of bacon cooking had dragged her out of a deep sleep. Half expecting a headache, she was relieved that no little man with his hammer was having a field day with her temples. She ran her tongue around her teeth and grimaced. "Ugh, furry mouth." The crumpled covers next to her were again evidence that someone had slept next to her but had now vacated the spot. Dredging up any memories of the last moments of the evening, she grinned. She recalled Taryn's gentle touch, as she peeled away her clothes. *Pity I was half cut, or I might have better memories.* She didn't recall much after she fell on the bed.

Her stomach growled as she climbed out of bed, and she shook her head. This town was going to play havoc with her waistline. Today, she had to do more exercise. She dragged on the T-shirt from the day before and pulled up jeans before opening the door. She heard talking and was unsure if it were Taryn speaking with Brenda, or the radio. She quickly used the toilet then brushed her teeth. A few minutes later, she tentatively went toward the delicious aroma coming from the kitchen.

Standing at the threshold, she saw Taryn at the stove and Brenda sitting at the table with the newspaper. "Morning."

Taryn turned with a bright smile. "Good morning. How did you sleep? Want some coffee? Breakfast should be ready shortly."

Brenda looked at her and rolled her eyes. "It's clear she isn't used to having company."

Logan moved into the room. "Mind if I sit?" Brenda only shrugged in response. "Thanks." She sat where she could see Taryn at the stove. The backside view was almost as good as the front—Taryn had one tight ass. "Breakfast smells good, what are we having?" She winked when Taryn turned to her.

"I'm an early riser, so I went to the store and bought some bacon and eggs, and I whipped up some pancakes to go with them." Her eyes widened. "Too much?"

"Sounds marvelous, but you really didn't need to do this for me. I feel like I'm taking advantage of your generosity. I would have happily taken you both out for breakfast." Logan looked at Brenda who shook her head and sneered.

"God no, not on our day off. Don't you think we get enough of that place? Besides it's closed today, and there's nowhere else to go," Brenda said.

Logan frowned. "Yeah, I forgot. Still, what about dinner? Surely there's a town nearby with a restaurant that's open."

"I bought a chicken to roast…we usually have that on Sundays, if I buy it and prepare it. I figured you'd join us?" Taryn gave a small smile.

Logan drew in a deep breath. "Guess I'm not going to win today on the food stakes. Although I insist tomorrow is my treat. Breakfast. Lunch. Dinner. Name it, or all of them." Inwardly, she groaned at the possibility of three meals in a day.

"We don't need someone feeding us like some charity case," Brenda spat out.

"Stop it." Taryn looked at Logan. "I'm sorry, that isn't how I feel. I'd love to go out to dinner with you tonight and all day tomorrow." She looked at Brenda. "You can have roast chicken alone."

"How dare you speak to me like that?" Brenda bellowed before slamming the paper on the table. "I'm going to take a bath and leave you two ingrates to yourselves."

Logan watched Brenda leave the room. "Well that went well. Your mother is mad at me again, and I thought I might have won her over with the porch. Guess not. Do you think we might be able to borrow her car again today, or is there anywhere we can hire one? The guy at the garage didn't offer, so I figured they didn't have anything."

"I'm sorry for how she acted. As for getting on her good side…she doesn't have one. I hope you did what you needed to in the bathroom, because she's likely to be in there all morning." Taryn walked over to the door. "As for the car…" She held up a set of keys and grinned. "Where would you like to go after we have some breakfast?"

Logan laughed. "Figured as the town is called Bourne Falls, you'd show me the falls. Or is that a misnomer?"

Taryn bit her lip. "The falls ceased to exist about fifty years ago, when they dammed the river fifteen miles upstream." She shrugged. "The swimming hole we were at is what's left. Not too many go out there anymore, because it got so overgrown with weeds. I usually ride my bike there, so the path is narrow and no one sees it. Hopefully, no one will notice the tire tracks we left and want to explore the area. I'd hate to share the place with anyone else."

"Ah, that explains it." Logan rubbed her hands together. "As much as I hate to say this, because all I seem to do here is eat, but I'm starving."

Taryn laughed. "Coming right up. I'm just about to turn the last pancake. Sorry, I forgot to buy syrup, but I do have honey."

"Perfect, then we will go out on our great big adventure together. I'm really looking forward to spending the next two days with you. We'll have a blast." Logan sat back in the chair and watched Taryn dish up the food.

"That would be like being in heaven." Taryn smiled shyly. "I've never cooked for anyone other than Brenda. I hope you like this." She set plates of scrambled eggs, bacon, and pancakes on the table.

Logan touched Taryn's hand and smiled. "Thanks, this looks delicious. And thank you for taking care of me last night. Maybe I need to sneak you in my suitcase when I leave here Tuesday." Logan watched Taryn sit and stare at her. "Something wrong?"

"If I thought you meant that I'd curl up inside your suitcase and go with you."

Logan chuckled. "Let's eat, and then we can start our adventure. Who knows? After two days together, I might just let you." She picked up her fork and began to eat.

"Who knows, indeed."

CHAPTER SEVEN

Taryn found it hard to drag her gaze away from Logan who stood in Brenda's kitchen in the same tight-fitting, black leather pants from the night before, a black T-shirt, and a black leather jacket. Again, hot was the only word she could use to describe how incredibly sexy the woman looked. She smoothed a hand down the leg of her shabby jeans.

"You're beautiful, Taryn." Logan took two steps closer and hugged her.

"Wanna go for that ride with me?"

"Best offer I've had all day. Let's go."

Taryn and Logan ran out of the house with the car keys in hand.

"Let's put the top down." Taryn unlocked the car and watched as Logan slid in beside her. Taryn started the car and pushed a button so that the rag top would go down. She flicked on the radio. "Find a station." The tires threw gravel behind them, as they set off for the famous Bourne Falls.

"Any preferences? I'm eclectic in my choices." Logan's hand reached for the dial.

"Something rocking that we can sing along with would be good."

Logan grinned. "Rocking works for me." Her fingers twisted the dial, and the sound of "Crazy" by Aerosmith blasted out of the speakers. "Will that work?"

"Definitely." Taryn cranked up the sound, and before long, they were both singing.

Ten minutes later, the car pulled into a neglected parking lot strewn with beer cans, cigarette butts, and condoms. "Welcome to our very own lover's lane and party spot." Taryn turned around, waving at what she could only describe as despicable. She looked at Logan. "Not what you expected is it?"

Logan jumped out of the car and walked over to a sign that said Bourne Falls Danger. "Maybe not, but I'm gonna have a picture taken here anyway." She removed a phone from her pocket and took a selfie. "Want me to take one with me and you?" She waved the silver phone in the air.

"Absolutely, I'm not wasting one minute with you." Taryn walked over and kissed Logan's cheek before putting her arm around her shoulders. "Smile."

Logan clicked the phone. "Great, our very first photo together." She turned to look at the overgrown area behind the sign. "Want to venture into danger with me?"

"Of course. Although I doubt anyone will hear us, if we tumble down the non-existent falls. Then again, no one will bother us either." She grabbed Logan's hand. "Come on, I remember a trail this way."

Together, they crept cautiously through the undergrowth. They stumbled only once on a well-placed rock and other debris. Taryn didn't mind, for Logan caught and held her for a minute before they continued. It wasn't but a couple of minutes, before dense greenery disappeared and the several trees dappled with sun greeted them. Birds were singing, and a slight breeze carried the scent of wild roses. They continued for another hundred yards before stopping in their tracks, when a steep decline came into view.

"Oh, what a pity," Logan said. "I bet this was a wonderful sight in its heyday." She turned to Taryn.

"I never got to see it, but my grandparents often spoke of having picnics here." Logan was so close that Taryn could feel her breath fanning her cheek. *It's now or never.* She leaned in and wrapped a hand around Logan's shoulders and pulled her close. "I want to kiss you," she whispered.

Logan leaned into Taryn and placed her lips on hers and began a slow exploration of Taryn's mouth. They eventually broke apart to breathe. Leaning her head against Taryn's, Logan whispered, "You're a great kisser."

Every emotion and feeling that Logan's kiss had brought to her the night before paled in comparison to what Taryn just felt. She wanted more. *Dare I?* "I had no idea…. Wow, kissing you makes my toes curl."

"Really? I like the sound of that." Logan smiled and drew her closer. "I'm very lucky." She kissed Taryn again, and their tongues locked.

The sensations coursing through her body caused Taryn to draw Logan closer. She had read enough books to know that what she was feeling was the want and need stories always lauded, but she had no idea that reality was so much better. When Logan's hand dropped to her hips and pulled her closer, all she could do was moan her pleasure and hope it would never stop.

"We have to stop," Logan said with a groan. "I don't want your first time to be out in the woods. It has to be special."

Before Taryn could say another word, the sound of car doors closing and the squeals of small children filled the air. "Why would anyone bring their kids here? Don't those parents know how dangerous it is?" Her arousal quickly dissipated, and she took a step back and blew out a breath. "The parking lot is strewn with condoms for God's sake."

"Maybe your mom and dad used to make out here." Logan chuckled. "Come on, let's go. What's next on our list?"

"Well, we can go to Sanderson Cross. It's a way better town than this place, and they have a decent mall if you're into that kind of thing."

"Sounds good. I saw something in the local paper I read yesterday that I want to check out. Thought I'd have to wait until my truck was repaired, but as we're going there, do you mind if we do that too?

"Not at all. Spending the day with you anywhere is nothing but icing on the cake." Taryn mentally slapped herself and laughed. "That was really corny, wasn't it?"

Logan laughed. "Yeah, but I like your version of corny. Sanderson Cross it is then." She snatched a chaste kiss, and they walked back, hand in hand, in the direction they'd come.

Someone had parked an old, beat up, yellow van next to Taryn's red convertible. "Guess they went on a hike." Taryn turned around in the parking lot. "This is so not a place to bring kids."

†

As Taryn drove down the main street of Sanderson Cross, it was clear to Logan that this town was thriving and had an understated excitement about it that Bourne Falls had lost or never even had. The buildings were brightly painted in so many different colors, she swore it could be an advert for the LGBT community to come visit or even stay. *I wonder if it is gay friendly?* People were milling around, doing whatever they had come out to do, and the billboards were all about community projects and the town. She noted that the population was thirty thousand, massive compared to the meagre one thousand in Taryn's hometown.

"Better than my town, isn't it?"

Taryn's voice sounded wistfully melancholy, and that wasn't surprising—not with a mother like Brenda who was always on her case and a town that had no sparkle. *Well, if I can bring a sparkle to Taryn's life for the short time I'm here, I'm going to do it.* Logan glanced at Taryn's profile, and her heart somersaulted. A sensation she had to admit was happening far more often than she'd expected.

"I don't know." She winked. "They don't have you in their town, do they?" Taryn shot her a beaming smile.

The car slowed as they came to a stoplight, and Logan continued her perusal of Sanderson Cross. Flowers in the colors of the US flag adorned concrete boxes every four buildings, and the flag itself flew from a pale-grey monument in the center. *Must be the original part of town.* The car made a right turn, and a few hundred yards later, the older style of the town gave way to new buildings before the mall came into view. Strangely enough, this small town had mastered the art of blending the old with the new, and it looked great.

"There must be money in Sanderson Cross. This is fantastic. Everything has been streamlined together." Logan smiled. She liked the vibe of the town and hadn't even got out of the car yet.

Taryn laughed. "Yeah, about twelve years ago, a couple of students at the college began an internet business and moved to California. Apparently, they made a ton of money when they sold out, and several of the investors were family members who live here. They used that wealth to reinvigorate the town. I wish someone could do that with Bourne Falls."

"Wow, that's what I call loving the place you live in. Have you thought about leaving Bourne Falls and getting a job here? Surely it has more prospects."

The car maneuvered into a parking spot, and Taryn stopped the vehicle. "Oh, how would I get a job here? I'm just a waitress, and if the places here pay anything like the Tavern, I'd be sleeping on the streets."

Logan considered that. She took Taryn's hand and held it tightly. "You sell yourself short. Don't forget you have another talent. I'm darn sure this town would love to have your art."

Taryn didn't say anything.

Logan slid over and straddled the gearshift before pulling her close and smiling. "I know, if I were a resident in this town, I would love to have such a talented person come live here." She then captured Taryn's lips and kissed her slowly. The sensation of tiny electric shocks going down her body surprised her as they had at the Falls. *Am I falling for this woman?* She pulled away slightly and watched the glazed expression in Taryn's eyes. *It definitely isn't one way, that's for sure. I can see it in her eyes.* "Let's go shopping. I'm sure there are things you can get here that you can't at home."

Taryn nodded and licked her lips.

Logan watched the slow process of the tongue, and her heart fluttered. If she could have crossed her legs at that moment she would have. *Damn, I'm going to have to take this woman to bed to get her out of my system.*

Climbing out of the car, Logan went around and opened the driver's door before holding out her hand. "Let's go shop."

Taryn smiled when Logan took her hand as they walked into the mall. Once inside, fear took hold of her. She only had thirty-three dollars and sixty-seven cents left after buying the breakfast items and that damn chicken. It would take nearly every bit of that to fill Brenda's gas hog to get them back to Bourne Falls. That didn't leave her very much if Logan wanted to have lunch. *Maybe if I persuade her to eat at Mickey D's, I can get a kid's meal for the remaining three dollars and change. God, I hate this.*

"Where do you want to go to first?" Logan asked.

"Um…well…the last time I was here was in my junior year of high school. Brenda needed a new dress. She took me along to distract the saleswoman, so she could steal some stockings. Needless to say, I only saw one store, Barnes Women's Clothing."

Logan looked around and pointed to the store. Taryn nodded. "Well, in that case, why don't we try Lucy's Merchandise for the Discerning Woman? Sound good? It's two doors down."

Taryn laughed. "You do know that the name is really lame, right?"

"Yeah, but sometimes a lame name has the best clothes. Come on, let's find out." Logan headed toward the store.

"Okay." Panic again filled Taryn, as she wondered how she'd pay for anything if Logan wanted her to buy something. "Um, I didn't help Brenda, so she never brought me again." She shrugged. "Just thought you should know."

Logan turned and grinned. "Good girl. Now come on, slowpoke, let's shop. I haven't been shopping with a girlfriend in years. and it will be a nice change from being on my own."

"I'm your girlfriend?" Taryn looked away, trying to disguise the pleasure she was feeling. She looked into

Logan's eyes and sighed before looking around the store. "What are you looking for? This doesn't seem like a store you'd go to."

"Sure, you are. You're a girl, right? And a friend? Makes sense to me. Quirky shops are interesting, and I love T-shirts. My mom used to say there weren't enough days of the year for all the ones I had when I lived at home. Look at those." Logan stepped over to the back wall and stared at the numerous printed tees.

"I bet I can pick out the one you'd like." Taryn looked over the assortment and pulled out a black T-shirt with a unicorn on it." She laughed. "How about this one?"

Taryn frowned knowing that she hadn't a clue about what Logan would like. She scrunched her face before chewing on the inside of her cheek puzzled by the sadness she suddenly felt.

Logan shook her head, laughing. "Hmm, maybe we need to get to know each other better. I like that one." Logan pointed to a white shirt with a rainbow arrow going through a red heart. "I'm going to the Chicago gay pride rally in two months. This will be perfect." She looked down at the pile of shirts with that motif, rummaging through it to find her size.

"What size?"

"Large. I like them roomy."

Taryn began sorting through a different pile and stopped when she saw the price tag. "Forty dollars? You've got to be kidding me."

"Hey, for quality and the right image that's cheap. Believe me, in the city it might be double that."

Taryn stood looking at Logan, knowing that her mouth was open and her eyes were bugging out. "Lucky for you that you have a grandmother who gave you money. It would take me working a full day to afford that shirt. If I did that, I wouldn't be able to eat anything other than what I get at the

Tavern. And that's only because Rosie likes me." She shook her head. "Unbelievable. I'll meet you outside when you're done."

Logan frowned and grabbed her arm. "They pay you forty bucks for a full day's work? Does that include tips?"

Taryn nodded.

"Girlfriend, you need a new job."

"Yeah, I know, you've said that before." Taryn walked out of the store.

Logan scowled. *Five dollars an hour?* "Is that even legal?" she mumbled. *When she waited tables, her employer had to supplement her salary when tips didn't bring her earnings up to minimum wage.* She let out a small snort. *That probably puts her at the poverty level. No wonder she's having a hard time getting out of that town.* She looked at the shirt in her hand and was about to put it back when a sales woman walked up to her.

"Great choice, it's one of our most popular shirts. We have a pride rally next week. Are you new in town?"

Logan was about to say she'd changed her mind, but the cheerful way the young woman spoke had her interested. "I didn't think a small town like this would be that engaging of the fringe minorities."

The girl laughed. "Not everyone in a small town is intolerant against different lifestyles. Besides, we are a medium-sized town. So, are you going to buy the shirt? What about that unicorn one for your girlfriend? I saw her eyes sparkle when she saw it?"

Hmm, not a bad idea. "Okay I'll take them both. Oh, give me a minute, I need to go check what size she needs."

The girl laughed. "You don't know her size? You must be on a first date then. My partner is about her size, and we do have a full-refund policy. Make it a surprise."

Logan grinned. "Sure, sounds like a plan."

A few minutes later, she headed out of the store and looked around for Taryn, who was sitting on bench across from Best Buy.

Logan held up her bag. "Got it. What's next? Want to go check out the new electronics? I heard they have virtual-reality goggles these days, and I'd love to try one out."

"I see you bought the T-shirt. It'll look great on you." She scowled. "Virtual-reality goggles? I hear those things cost a hundred dollars." She shrugged. "Sure, let's go look at them." Taryn started to walk toward the store and stopped. "Sorry about making a scene in that store."

Logan smiled. "You didn't make a scene. You had an opinion, and I respect that." Logan had to stop herself from grinning like a Cheshire cat when Taryn's eyes bulged as they entered the store. "Don't you just love these places?" She took Taryn's hand and dragged her toward a display of the gadget she'd heard her friends talk about.

Logan dropped Taryn's hand and picked up one of the boxes to read the details. "Want to try one? They have a display model."

"It looks like it needs something at the front."

"Hmm, you could be right." Logan looked around and saw a sales person. She waved the man over. "Can we try this out?"

"Yep, let me find the app on my phone. Really cool concept. I bought one myself."

Logan turned to Taryn and winked. She wasn't sure if Taryn was excited about trying out the new technology, but at least she could say she'd had a whole new experience.

"Here you go. Just move these buttons on the side as you view." He was about to hand her the goggles, and she waved her hand at Taryn. "Ladies first."

Taryn took the device and placed it over her eyes. She wasn't sure what to expect. "Okay, what now?"

"Where would you like to go?" the guy asked.

"Um, Niagara Falls."

"Great choice."

The next thing Taryn knew, she was standing next to a gigantic waterfall. "I've never seen anything like it." Suddenly the water was rushing past her, and she was walking to the edge of the falls. "Logan, you should see this. It's unbelievable." Her stomach started to roil at the motion. "I think I've seen enough."

The salesperson stopped the app. "You can take them off now."

When Taryn opened her eyes, she saw a beaming Logan who came over to her and gave her a hug. "You should try it."

"I'm going to." She took the goggles from Taryn.

"Where would you like to go?"

"A field of sunflowers on a rainy day." Logan grinned, as Taryn chuckled.

"Hmm, not sure that's possible." The salesperson frowned and then smiled. "Would a storm be okay?"

"Sure, go for it." Logan's head jerked back almost as soon as she put the goggles on.

"Wow…wow…oh my god. I want one of these." Moments later, she removed the goggles and her smile beamed.

"No worries there. We have three in stock."

Logan shrugged. "Oh, I think they might be out of my price range."

"I can find out if we have a special price." The assistant waited.

Logan looked at Taryn who frowned. "Let me think about it. If I decide to purchase it, I'll surely come here to buy."

The man shrugged and wished them a good morning and went off in the direction of an elderly couple looking at laptops.

"I thought you might be suckered in," Taryn said, as she stood shuffling around beside Logan.

"These places really make you nervous, don't they?"

Taryn chewed on her lip and looked away. "Is it that obvious?"

Logan nodded.

"You've seen where I live and now know how little I make. I get nervous, because I know I can never have the money to just buy stuff like that." She lifted a shoulder. "I know I need to get out of there, but I never can get ahead enough to make the move. Does that make sense to you?"

Logan took Taryn's arm and hugged her close. "Perfect," she whispered. "Let's go have a delicious coffee at The Beanery, one of my fav franchises at home. My treat."

"I'd like that. Thank you."

†

Taryn looked around the coffee shop. She'd seen them on TV but had never actually been in one. There were three people drinking coffee and working on laptops. A young woman was drinking what looked like a cup of coffee while idly moving a stroller. Several couples were also there, along with five people sitting alone.

91

"Here you go. Black one sugar." Logan held out the paper cup with a cardboard wrapper around the middle and steam coming from the lid.

"Thanks." Taryn took a sip of the coffee and bit her lip. "I saw that this cost five dollars, but I think the coffee at the Tavern is just as good. It only costs a dollar with unlimited refills." She gave Logan a quizzical look. "I don't get it."

Logan chuckled as she sat. "Well, it's all about ambiance. Could you see people sitting in the tavern working on laptops? Take that woman relaxing with her baby, indulging in a treat that she probably doesn't have time to do at home. Sometimes it isn't about the money but the quality of the moment."

"I hadn't thought of it that way." Taryn sighed and shook her head. "Truth be told, I'm jealous of them—of you—that you can come into a place like this or that shop and buy whatever you want without a second thought. I just wish I could say it isn't about the money. I guess it's easier to say that when you have money."

"What do you mean?"

"I have a savings account of two hundred and ten dollars. If I'm lucky, after taxes, I take home less than two hundred dollars a week if the tips are good. I pay Brenda a hundred dollars a week to live in her rat hole, along with an extra ten if I use my welder. And I'm the one who buys the food. That doesn't leave me much for things like a five-dollar coffee." Taryn let out a sarcastic laugh. "Of course, Brenda would be in here in a heartbeat if it was in Bourne Falls."

Logan reached out and took her hand. "Maybe it's time you moved on. I really do mean that."

Taryn closed her eyes. "I know I need to get out of there, but don't you see? I'm trapped, Logan. I don't earn enough to leave." She heard Logan sigh and wondered if she'd finally pissed her off.

"I've not always had money, Taryn. In fact, what my grandmother left me is all I have. I had a job in the city that paid well enough, but I worked long, unsociable hours. Like you, my apartment took pretty much half of what I earned. I was fortunate to have decent meals at my folks' place three times a week, until they left the state. It isn't easy out there, I know. Yes, I spend money on what you think is frivolous, but it's what makes me get up to go to work—treating myself from time to time—otherwise I'd be a basket case. I also had a credit card. It wasn't maxed out, but it was a big relief when Grams left me an inheritance, and I could pay it off."

Logan continued holding her hand. "I'm a big believer in that everyone can change what they have to something better, if they need to. The big question is deep inside." Logan gently placed a finger at Taryn's chest. "You have to want to, regardless of the risks. Life is risk. We can walk out of here and get run over or something like that." Logan smiled and pulled Taryn's hand towards her lips and kissed it. "You can dream of the knight in shining armor to get you out of the hole you are in *or*, you can do it yourself. That's the choice you must make. Sorry if that's not what you wanted to hear." Logan picked up her coffee and sipped it.

Taryn wiped away a lone tear that coursed down her cheek. "How did I get so lucky to have you come into my life?" She squeezed Logan's hand. "Will you help me find a way out?"

†

"Why are you so cagey about this place we're going to, Logan?"

Logan grinned and pulled Taryn along the street. She stopped so suddenly that Taryn bumped into her. The reaction her body had at the contact caught at the back of her throat. She closed her eyes for a few seconds then turned to Taryn. "We're here."

"Where? It's the middle of the street." Taryn frowned and turned in a circle.

Logan turned Taryn again in her arms. "What do you think?" Logan held her breath.

Taryn gazed at the building, and scratched the top of her head. "I don't understand."

"It's for sale, a café, and exactly what I was looking for." Logan's excitement deflated at Taryn's confusion.

"You might buy this?" Taryn's eyes were wide.

"I saw it advertised in the local paper, and with a bit of a squeeze, it's in my price range to buy the property. It's in the old town part, I know, but I think this town is going places. Besides, I don't want to earn millions, but it would be nice to get up each day and go to work for myself doing something I like. What do you really think?" Logan saw several expressions cross Taryn's face, and she wasn't sure what they meant.

"Will you need a waitress when you open your café?" Taryn raised her eyebrows. "I've had some experience in that area."

Logan grinned. "You'd be my first choice. What's your first impression from the outside? I think it looks quaint, and a new paint job would work wonders." She placed her hands around the window and peered inside the darkened interior.

"I think it is great. Do you think we can get someone to show us inside? Brenda had me clearing tables when I was ten, so I will know what works." Taryn looked at Logan.

Logan moved away from the glass and reached inside her pocket to pull out a piece of newsprint. "I'm sure the phone number is on here, and the ad said call anytime." She drew out her phone and punched in a number. "Let's hope they take the call." She winked at Taryn.

Taryn smiled broadly. "I'm so excited for you."

Logan grinned, then a voice said "Hello." She pressed the speaker button and held the phone out. "This is Sally Meyers. How may I help you?"

"Hi, I saw your advertisement for Sally's Bistro and wondered if there was a chance you could show me around. I'm actually in town today and outside the building."

"Oh, right. Well, I'm in the middle of making lunch for my kids, but I can meet you there in an hour, if that's okay."

Logan smiled. "Sounds great. I'm Logan Perry."

"Excellent, Logan. I'm Sally. It's my place, so I know everything about it." The sound of children bickering in the background had Taryn chuckle. "See you in an hour. Got to go. The kids get antsy when they're hungry."

"Bye." Logan disconnected the call. "Guess we're going to get a tour. Want to have lunch? I'm suddenly starving. Oh, and before you frown, this day is on me. That includes all the travelling costs. No argument. Okay?" She placed a finger to Taryn's lips and then gave her a swift, gentle kiss.

Taryn blew out a breath. "Thank god for that. I was wondering how I was going to pay for gas and lunch. How about you pay for lunch and I pay for the gas?"

Logan wagged her finger and gave her a mock stern look. "Nope, my treat. And don't think it's charity. Staying at your place is more than compensation. You choose where to go, and don't go for the cheap menu place." Logan took Taryn's hand, as they wandered down the street.

Taryn looked around the area and pointed to a place called Big Belly Burgers on the corner. "Shall we see what the competition has to offer?"

"Sounds like a plan to me. It looks like the only place to eat around here. Looks full too."

"Let's go, and as you're paying, I'm going to have the biggest burger and all the trimmings they have, with large fries and a Coke."

Logan shook her head and laughed, as they crossed the road to the burger joint.

†

Taryn bumped hips with Logan, as they stood in front of the vacant café. "That was a decent burger, although it seemed to take forever to get served. One thing Rosie always told me is to keep the customers happy you have to get the food out to them fast."

"Yeah, they were pretty slow. Did you notice that no one smiled at the counter, like it was a major chore to be at work? I don't want that when I own a place of my own." Logan shook her head and shrugged.

"There is nothing worse than an unhappy customer…believe me, I know." Taryn looked up when she saw a white Ford Explorer pull to the curb in front of the café. Two young kids were screaming in the backseat. "Wow, no wonder she had to give up the café."

Logan laughed. "Got to say, kids are not on my list of must haves, what about you?"

"With a mother like Brenda, what do you think?" Taryn grinned. A stout woman with blonde hair and a frazzled look got out of the vehicle. "Hi, ladies, I'm Sally. Which one of you is Logan?"

Logan shot out her hand. "I'm Logan, and this is my friend, Taryn. Glad you could make the time at such short notice.

"Are you kidding? I haven't had any interest in the place since I put it on the market last July. Oh yeah, I shouldn't have said that. My husband would have the largest frown in history on his face right now." She rummaged in her bag and withdrew a set of keys. "Let's get you two ladies inside and see what you think. I'll be as honest as I can, but the place hasn't been trading for a year, so the figures I give will be out of date."

"No, problem." Logan grinned at Taryn, as they entered the building.

Taryn looked around. The place was a reasonable size with bistro tables and chairs that looked to be in good condition. The floor was dusty, and it made her appreciate the Tavern owner's insistence on cleanliness. She looked at Logan who nodded and asked, "What type of café was this, Sally?"

"I guess you would call it a coffee house. My specialty was pastries and donuts. People came from miles away, every morning, for bags of my bagels too. I miss it, but with two preschoolers it was too much. Especially with my hyper kids."

"Yeah, they seem feisty." Logan smiled, her eyes going to the direction of the car.

"Feisty is one word for it, that's for sure. Love 'em, but they are hard work. My husband has a job in Fresno, and we are moving there to be with him in a couple of months. Go have a good scout around, and then ask me anything you want. I'll just go out and check on the kids and my sister. She might end up murdering them." Sally smiled and went out the door.

"What do you think?" Logan said.

"Let's see what the kitchen is like. This part needs paint and ambience, but the kitchen is the heart of any food place." Logan took her hand, and they wandered into the kitchen. "Would you look at that." Taryn eyed the ten-burner gas top, with a large grill and two convection ovens, lined against one wall. "This is all high-end stuff, for the most part."

"The coffee machine isn't up to scratch, but I know the perfect machine for a place like this. So that's an easy replacement," Logan said.

"If I owned a restaurant, this is the kitchen I'd want. Sally spared no expense in this kitchen." Taryn looked out the back door. "I wonder if that building comes with the place."

Logan looked in the direction Taryn pointed. "Wow, that's almost as big as the floor space inside here. I don't see a fence or anything separating it from this building, and see, there's another smaller building as well."

Sally came into the kitchen. "Anything I can help you with?"

"Are those buildings out the back part of the sale?" Logan asked.

"Yeah, I never used the big barn, although it's sound. The smaller unit was great for keeping supplies, even had a refrigeration unit added. There's a small apartment upstairs, not very big, but for a single person or even a couple, it would be okay. Want to see it?" Sally gave them a long look.

Logan frowned, and Taryn quickly said, "No, it's okay for the moment."

"The advertisement said you wanted two hundred thousand to buy the place outright. Is that right?" Logan softly asked.

Sally nodded. "Yeah, that's right."

Taryn looked at Logan in question, and when she saw her wink and nod, she turned to Sally. "Considering the neighborhood and all what was your clientele like? What was the median age, and what sold the best or not at all?"

"Oh, most folks who came have lived here all their lives, but I started to have a few younger folks turning up on weekends, mainly for coffee. That side of the business was really taking off. They used to ask me for all different kinds of coffee. To be honest, I didn't have a clue. Anyway, going back to the original question, the age group was probably mid-thirties upwards. Of course, the bagel run was all ages. Bagels were my best-selling item, and my morning pastries sold second best. Honestly, I never really had anything that didn't sell."

"Sounds interesting. Did you always compete with the burger place down the street?" Logan asked.

"Not for the first two years. The youngsters mainly go there, and it didn't really interfere with my profits. In fact, it probably helped. I hear the service isn't that great, and my service was always friendly and prompt. Never had any complaints there." She shrugged. "It's like comparing apples to oranges. What I sold here wasn't something they sold."

"Well thanks, Sally, for showing us around. I'm not from around here and saw it by chance, so I need to think it over." Logan held out her hand, and Sally shook it as she did Taryn's hand.

As they left the building, Sally smiled. "It was a pleasure to meet you both. If you really are interested, I might be able to do something on the price, so let me know." She waved as she climbed into the vehicle and seconds later shot off down the street.

"What do you think?" Logan turned to Taryn.

"Are you serious about this?"

"You know, when I saw the ad it screamed at me. Now after seeing the town and all it has to offer, this place is calling my name. Can't really explain it, but I like this town. I'd be happy to live here, I think. I know I'm a city girl, but this offers me so many opportunities. So yep, I'm serious about this. She might bring down the price, especially since she wants to move in a few months."

"In that case, I think that this is a good location. I know all I've known of restaurants is in Bourne Falls, but I've listened to Rosie over the years. She knows her stuff. She'd kill for a kitchen like that. If I had the money, I'd buy it."

"Well in that case, let's go wandering and see the rest of the place. I have a feeling in my bones. This was all meant to be. My gran would be proud." Logan chuckled, as she took Taryn's hand while they wandered down the street.

Taryn smiled, as she walked with Logan. The people at the Tavern only ever asked her what was on special and never wanted her opinion of what was good or not. Logan not only wanted her opinion but encouraged her. *This is turning out to be a really great day.*

Logan glanced back, as they walked away from the building. *I'm crazy. Totally crazy. I love living in Chicago. Yet...this is the place. I feel it inside.* She looked at Taryn, who was smiling. *No, it isn't this woman's influence.* A voice inside her head asked *why not. I've always wanted to work for myself, that's why.*

"Well, we know about Big Belly Burgers, so let's check out as many other eateries as we can, if you're serious."

"Thank you for this. I'm sure you wanted this to be a fun day. I'm sorry—"

Taryn put a finger over her lips. "No. Never be sorry, Logan. Whatever we do together is fun." Taryn squeezed her hand. "Besides, if you do buy the café, there's a chance that I can actually move on. That is something, until today, I never thought could be possible. Thank you."

Logan smiled and pulled Taryn close. "Whatever I chose to do, I'm thankful I met you."

"Me too. Now come on, let's see if we can make a go of this. I now have a vested interest."

Logan's heart swelled. *Is it really that simple?* "Yeah, let's go."

CHAPTER EIGHT

"I had no idea this town had so many restaurants. What is your opinion?"

Logan scowled. "Hmm, maybe it wasn't such a good idea. Possibly too much competition." Logan settled back against a low wall running down the main street.

"I don't agree. Other than the coffee shop we went to this morning, we didn't see anything like it in all the places we visited." Taryn reached out and touched Logan's hand. "Rosie has always told me that the secret to success in restaurants is to give the masses what they want." She shrugged. "I think you can do that."

"Mass coffees?" Logan chuckled. "I can do that."

"Yes, you can." Taryn sat next to Logan. "Years ago, when I was five or six, my grandparents brought me here. We went to a place called Sanderson's Peak. It's just outside of town, and as I remember, we had to drive in a circle up the mountain. At the top is a platform where you can see three hundred and sixty degrees. I remember being mesmerized by what I saw."

"Well, that sounds great. Shall we go? I love those scenic areas. One day, I'm going to go to the Grand Canyon, but that will have to be the next trip." Logan grinned and stretched her body like a cat.

†

Thirty minutes later, Taryn and Logan stood side by side on the observation deck. "Look over there," Taryn said pointing to the north. "See the river and the dam? If you continue in that direction, you can see where the falls were and after that the town."

Logan stared at the scene below her and the fast running river. Boulders splattered along the route caused the river to crest in white waves. Looking at the horizon, she could make out the dam and, in the far distance, Taryn's home town. With the clear blue sky above, this was certainly a peaceful and lovely place to spend some time. "I'd call this majestic and a place to reflect. Do you know what else?" She looked directly at Taryn.

"No, I don't."

Logan laughed and pointed to the large parking area. "We could have a stall here selling coffees, if we find out it's a tourist trap."

Taryn grinned. "You do have a point there. We'll have to investigate the traffic that comes up here." She pointed to the parking area. "Right now, we'd be the only ones buying coffee."

"Hey, you have to start somewhere." Logan pulled Taryn into her arms and kissed her slowly. As they broke apart, she whispered, "I feel like I'm alive again and making plans for the future. I haven't done that since Lindy left me. Thank you."

"Wanna tell me about it?"

"Are you interested? I don't want to bore you." Logan stared at the flowing river below.

Taryn wrapped her arms around Logan and pulled her close. "I want to know everything about you, Logan. The good, the bad, and the ugly."

Logan snuggled close. "I met Lindy my last year in college. She was ten years older than me and came to campus to give a lecture on the food chain business. I was taking a degree in business studies, so it fit. That and it was raining and there was only that auditorium open. I fell for her the moment I set eyes on her. She was a willowy brunette with generous breasts and a smile that lit up a room." Logan felt Taryn squirm. "Are you sure you want to hear this?"

"Yes, yes I do."

"Anyway, to cut a long story short, fate had it that we ended up sharing a table in the refectory, and we hit it off. After I graduated, she offered me a job in her small restaurant. That's how I learned about coffee making, among other things. I was the best barista in town. We lived together for three years. One day, she packed my bag and told me to get out, because she'd found someone else. I was devastated."

"Ouch. I can't believe anyone would do something like that to you of all people." Taryn pulled her close. "You are so kind and generous. Why would she do something like that?" A small laugh came from Taryn. "Is it okay that if I ever meet her I'll scratch her eyes out?"

Logan smiled. "That would be okay, though usually that's my job, being butch and all. Not that you'd know it these days."

"I think you are wonderful. Thank you for sharing that with me. As for the butch part, I think you are perfect the way you are."

"You know, I should have listened to my mom. She told me Lindy was a player, but I didn't believe it. You don't know something like that when you fall in love and everything seems perfect. No one is, for sure, I'm not. Still, I lost interest in the business and moved from job to job. I guess I didn't want to meet up with her one day if we were in the same industry. My gran dying and leaving me a decent inheritance was the catalyst to getting off my butt and doing something with my life. Here I am." Logan sighed and turned in Taryn's arms and kissed her gently.

Taryn had never felt the way she did at that moment in Logan's arms. The kiss was soft and gentle, holding what she thought was a silent promise. She knew that her time with Logan was limited. She'd leave in a few days. *I'll make the most of it.* She deepened the kiss, trying to pour all the feelings she had for Logan into her lips and tongue.

When they broke apart, Logan rested her head against Taryn's forehead. "How about we go back to your place and explore these feelings we have for each other?"

"I'd like that." Taryn's lips sought out Logan's before pulling away. "With any luck, Brenda will be out with one of her many guys."

"Surely, she can't be that bad. You don't have the population in Bourne Falls for her to have lots of guys. Some of them must be happily married." Logan grinned, as she took Taryn's hand to turn back to the car.

"You'd be surprised at how many randy men are in Bourne Falls. Married or not, I can't think of one who hasn't shared her bed at least once." Taryn laughed. "Brenda just can't say no."

"Maybe she's lonely. Can't have been easy being the wife of the most vilified man in town. I don't mean any disrespect to your dad, just relating the things you told me."

"My dad was defending himself, but the town only saw the jobs lost." Taryn chewed on her lip. "Maybe she is lonely. I don't know. What I do know is that she drinks too much and will screw any guy that comes along." She gave Logan a small smile. "Enough about her. I seem to recall you saying something about exploring feelings."

"Indeed, I did."

Taryn took Logan's hand and led her down the steps to the ground and to the red convertible. Once they were sitting in the car, she leaned over and kissed Logan. She pulled away, breathless. "It's usually a thirty-minute drive. Shall we see if we can make it in twenty?"

"Absolutely."

†

Taryn pulled the car up in front of the house and gasped.

A furious looking Brenda came flying out of the house, her sheer negligee fluttering around her ample body. She flung the driver's door open. "Get the hell out of my car. How dare you steal it while I was taking a bath." She glared at Logan. "You're responsible for this. Get out of my car and out of my house."

Taryn stepped out of the car and went toe to toe with Brenda. "The deal was, if I took your Saturday night shift I could use your car. I kept my part of the bargain, and now you're reneging on our agreement."

"I didn't say you could use it all weekend just that one time."

"So, now you're changing the rules? I don't think so."

Brenda pointed at Logan, who had come around the car and was standing next to Taryn. "Get out of my house and away from my daughter, you dyke."

"No, she will not leave. She is my guest, and as long as I pay you rent, I can have anyone in my room that I want. Unless you want me to leave as well. Then who'd pay you rent for that rat hole? Where would that leave you? No more expensive negligees for your men friends, that's for sure."

Logan watched the mother and daughter explosion. Sure as hell, that's exactly what it was. *Is this all my fault?* She stared at the pair, who looked like they were about to go ten rounds in a ring. "Look, if this will stop any fracturing of a mother-daughter relationship, then I'm gone and I apologize for creating this problem."

Taryn turned to her, and Logan almost melted at the anguish in her expression. Brenda was another proposition altogether—her face looked like thunder and victory.

"You can get off my property now. Look what you've done, turning my daughter against me."

The accusations were unfounded, but for Brenda this was probably just another person to blame for her problems. Logan wasn't a psychiatrist, but it had been clear since the moment they met. "I will, Brenda." She held up her arms. "No one is causing trouble. In fact, your daughter has been invaluable to me, regarding the business arena within the next fifty miles. Truth be told, I'm looking to invest in a business close by."

"You are? What type of business?"

"A coffeehouse in Sanderson Cross with lots of prospects and, if it works out, jobs too." *Okay that was shameless, but it worked.* Brenda's expression was interested.

"Work in Sanderson Cross, are you serious?"

Logan turned to Taryn and placed her arm over her shoulder. "Taryn was wonderful, giving me lots of tips and great ideas. I like the prospect."

Brenda frowned. "You have money?"

"Sure, doesn't everyone outside Bourne Falls? I'm from Chicago, the land of plenty. Anyway, thank you for your hospitality. How much do you want for my stay here?"

Logan saw Taryn about to respond and gently squeezed her shoulder.

Brenda clutched her hands together. "Hundred dollars until you leave…in advance."

Logan smiled and withdrew her wallet. She extracted a hundred-dollar bill and held it in the air. "Okay, but we get the use of the car until I leave."

"That's highway robbery."

"Take it or leave it."

"Fine."

Logan handed over the bill. "Here you go."

Brenda clutched the bill and sneered at Taryn. "Do what you want, but don't waste the opportunity." She retreated to the house.

Taryn could feel the anger she'd been holding back all her life bubble to the surface, threatening to explode. Logan had just handed a hundred-dollar bill to Brenda, and that wasn't right. For as long as she remembered, Brenda had used her to get her way. Taryn accepted her complicity in that, but she would not allow Brenda to use her friend. Not by a long shot. "Why did you do that? I can have anyone I want stay with me in the room *I* pay for." She looked at Logan and shook her head. "I'm going to get your money back."

"No, let her have the money. I can afford it, and if it means she gets off your back, then I'm more than happy. Besides, we have free rein of the car until I leave. Works for me. What about you?"

Taryn couldn't help but smile. Logan's infectious, positive approach was rubbing off on her. "Okay then. Tell me what you'd like to do next? Go swimming?"

"Sure, we can't exactly have any private time with your mother in the house, especially now I know exactly how she feels about me. Let's go. Maybe, just maybe I can heat you up in another way." Logan snatched a kiss.

The thought of seeing Logan naked sent chills up and down her spine. "I'm ready if you are." They were just getting back in the car, when Brenda came out of the house.

"Where the hell do you think, you're going?" she screamed. "I need my car."

"A deal's a deal, Brenda," Taryn threw over her shoulder, as the GTO sped away with the occupants laughing.

†

The sun was still shining, although the light wouldn't last much longer.

Logan stretched her body and relished the moment, as Taryn's slim fingers moved over her belly. They had indulged in a lengthy swim and some delectable horseplay. She hadn't played Blindman's Touch since high school. Closing her eyes and touching Taryn, and describing what she touched, was a more pleasurable experience than when she was fifteen and all fumbles and embarrassment. This had been a delicate exploration without intrusion, giving her a way to know how Taryn would react to a more intense situation like making love. The cold water helped in cooling her own intensity and quenching the fire in her body, somewhat. Taryn's responses had been eager and genuine. She was ready to take that final step. Did Logan have the heart to do that and then walk away without a care?

Taryn's fingers stopped when they skimmed across the bottom of Logan's breast. She let out an audible groan. "I want to know what it's like to feel your breasts," she whispered. "Is that okay?"

"Are you sure? I don't know that I can stop myself from doing the same or more. Passion is a tempting mistress." Logan propped herself up on her left arm and stared at Taryn, needing to see if this freaked her out. Apparently not, as Taryn leaned in and kissed her hard, their tongues intertwining. When they broke apart, Logan deftly removed Taryn's bra and underwear before taking her own off. She lay on her side, looking down at Taryn's naked body. She took in a deep breath and closed her eyes, feeling the passion in her body crying out for release. She kissed the waiting lips.

"God, I can't believe this is happening to me," Taryn whispered when they broke apart. With shaking fingers, she reached out and ran her thumb over one of Logan's hardened nipples. The sensation that one touch spread throughout her body was like nothing she'd ever experienced before. When Logan's hand rested on the back of her head, encouraging her to go further, she wasted no time in tasting what she'd been dreaming about since she'd met the woman. Logan groaned and held Taryn's head firmly in place as she greedily sucked the nipple.

"Are you sure this is what you want?" Logan's ragged voice asked.

"Yes, since the moment we touched in the water," was Taryn's breathless reply. "Please, Logan, teach me."

Logan lifted on one arm, before she lay on top of Taryn, moving so one of her breasts was in the valley of Taryn's and one leg was resting between her legs. "First, we have to feel each other's body. How does this feel to you?"

"Like heaven. Is this what being turned on feels like?"

"It is only the beginning. I want to make love with you, Taryn." Logan leaned and gave her a kiss that was full of promise of what was to come. "If I do anything you don't like, tell me. Okay?"

"Okay, but I doubt there is anything I won't like. Please, make love to me."

The sound of voices off in the distance had them scrambling up and quickly putting on their clothes.

"I thought you said no one else comes here." Logan was pulling on her shoes.

"I've never seen a sign of anyone else being here, but I've never been here this late."

"Come on. Let's go back to the house. We need to eat. Don't know about you, but I'm famished. What the heck do you put in the water here? I never eat this much at home." Logan grinned.

They ran for the car, and Taryn started it up just as a brown Jeep flew by before turning away from the water.

"Assholes," Taryn mumbled.

CHAPTER NINE

Logan hesitated for a brief second before entering the house behind Taryn, who hung up the car keys and then headed into the kitchen. She was unclear if Brenda would be there, and another confrontation right now wasn't what she wanted. Nope, she wanted to experience the emotions of making love to Taryn. Although their earlier attempt was interrupted, it was nonetheless exciting, eliciting feelings she hadn't experienced since Lindy left. The more she thought about the prospect of bedding Taryn, the more she craved doing so, even in the kitchen. That was totally unlike her, and a part of her felt foolish and schoolgirlish.

"Hey, slowpoke don't you want to check out my cooking skills?" Taryn's head popped out from behind the kitchen doorway, her lips twisted in a wonderful smile.

I'm beginning to wonder who is more turned on in this relationship, me or Taryn. "Yeah, I'm coming." She entered the kitchen and blew out a breath. Brenda wasn't around, at least not in the kitchen. "Brenda's not around?"

Taryn sneered and glanced at the clock on the wall. "She probably got a lift to her poker game. It's alternate houses, and we played host last week."

"Men or women, or shouldn't I ask?"

Taryn snickered but didn't turn to look at Logan, as she withdrew a chicken from the fridge. "Mixed crowd, usually they end up arguing. I go out to my shop and work on a Sunday, works for all of us."

"Oh, am I stopping you from doing something important? It's okay if you want to go into your workshop. I can watch TV until you're done."

Taryn dropped the utensil she was holding and ran around the kitchen table and pulled Logan into her arms. She kissed her softly, then whispered, "Not a chance. We have unfinished business." She gently bit Logan's earlobe. With a saucy wink, she went back to her preparation of the chicken.

Logan grinned as she stared at Taryn's back, but her hackles rose, as a voice filled with bitterness spoke behind her.

"You took your time getting back. What if I needed my car for something important?"

Logan sucked in a deep breath and turned to Brenda, as she saw Taryn's back arch. "Yes, Taryn figured you might need it this evening, and she didn't want you walking to your poker game."

"Yeah, right." Brenda snorted. "What are you doing, Taryn?"

Taryn switched around and gave her mother a deep stare. "Dinner, it will be ready in two hours."

"Well that's too late for me, why didn't you get home earlier?"

"Are you kidding me? Brenda, you can cook as well as me. Why didn't you have it ready for me."

Brenda scowled. "I'd rather give it to the dog than make a dinner for you and that…" she turned to pierce Logan with a glare. "You are going to be hurt, Taryn. Mark my words. She's only going to use you then discard you, like they all do after they get their way."

Taryn opened her mouth, but obviously couldn't articulate and closed it.

"What way would that be, Brenda?" Logan asked with a faint smile.

"Sex. That's what you want. I saw you two kissing. You'll leave her in this hellhole, like every one of your kind do. Believe me, I know all about that. False promises about a job in Sanderson Cross, my ass."

Logan bit her upper lip then spoke. "I see, so you have experience with lesbian lovers as well as men. Wow."

Taryn chuckled, and Logan smiled wider.

"Don't be disgusting. I don't sleep with women. I'm getting out of here, but mark my words, Taryn. She's gonna hurt you, big time, and don't come to me looking for sympathy. Mine all dried up when your dad died." She left the doorway.

Logan heard the jangle of keys and the front door opening and then slamming shut.

"Again, that went well." Logan shrugged and walked over to Taryn, who was placing the chicken in the oven. She wrapped her arms around Taryn's stomach. "However, she has left. So how about we use that two hours to get to know each other better."

Taryn turned in her arms and smiled. Logan's heart somersaulted, and she was lost in a kiss that melted every single thought that this might not be a good move.

"Take me to bed please," Taryn hoarsely whispered.

Logan lifted Taryn into her arms and swiftly walked to the bedroom they were sharing, kicking the door shut behind them.

Taryn looked at Logan who was sitting on the bed and patting it for Taryn to come and sit by her. She blushed and said, "Can you give me a minute to go to the bathroom?"

Logan smiled. "Sure. Don't be long."

"I won't." Taryn hurried out the door, went into the bathroom, and closed the door behind her, resting against it. Taking a deep breath, she went to the sink and brushed her teeth before quickly running a wash cloth over her body. If this was going to be her first time, and potentially her last time with Logan, she wanted to at least be clean.

When Taryn opened the door to her bedroom, her eyes widened and she gasped at Logan lying on the bed naked. Her body was reacting in the way now familiar whenever she was anywhere near Logan. Her fingers fumbled on the doorknob, before they found the lock and twisted it.

"I missed you," Logan's sultry voice said. "Come join me."

With tentative steps, Taryn walked the short way to the bed and stood beside it.

"Take your clothes off."

Taryn looked directly into Logan's eyes while removing her clothes and saw what she thought was desire. Naked, she crawled onto the narrow bed, lying on her back next to Logan. She could feel her heart thumping hard. "Logan, I don't—"

A slender finger pressed against her lips. "Let me show you."

Logan moved so that her thigh was between Taryn's legs, before lips replaced the finger.

Taryn found herself lost in a tender, sensual kiss, while Logan's thigh pressed against her center.

Logan lifted her head and smiled before nibbling on Taryn's ear. "Do you like that?'

"Oh, yes."

"And, this?" Logan kissed her neck.

"Yes," she whispered.

"And this?' Logan ran her tongue over a nipple.

"Yes, please don't stop." Taryn held Logan's head in place not wanting the sensations her body was feeling to stop—they didn't.

In her wildest dreams, Taryn never thought anything could feel as good as what Logan's mouth and thigh were doing to her. She heard herself groan in pleasure, when Logan's fingers twisted her other nipple. "Oh, god."

Logan's hand snaked between them, and Taryn had to close her eyes when she felt the finger slide along her center. The feelings that touch evoked made her lift her hips, begging and wanting more. When Logan's lips left her breast, her eyes flew open. "Did I do something wrong?" She could hear the desperation in her voice.

"No, you're doing everything right." Logan smiled down at her before beginning to place feather light kisses down her stomach. She stopped briefly to swirl her tongue in Taryn's belly button before descending further.

Taryn swallowed hard when Logan's lips began sucking her in the most pleasurable place, just as a finger slid inside her. She had read about making love, but her wildest imaginings didn't compare to what her body was feeling at that moment. It was like a dark room that finally filled with light. For the first time, Taryn could see all the wonders of that room. Her hips began moving in time with Logan, and soon she found herself floating high above the world with pleasure coursing through her body. With one last gasp, she

116

grabbed the sheets, before her body shuddered in an explosion of desire. Taryn lay there sated and, for the first time in her life, gloriously happy.

The next thing Taryn knew, lips were kissing her, while tears of happiness leaked out of the corners of her eyes. Her hand gently caressed Logan's cheek. "I had no idea. Please, let me love you." With a tentative move, she began kissing toward Logan's breasts. As her confidence grew, she twisted one nipple while sucking the other. Logan's hand took hers and snaked it between their bodies. With a finger on top of hers, Logan pressed hard on a nub that Taryn felt before circling it. Logan guided her fingers through velvety wet folds and gently slid one of Taryn's fingers inside. When she did, Logan removed her hand and began rocking her hips.

With the memory of what Logan had done to bring her to orgasm, Taryn slipped in another finger and began pumping. When she felt a tightening around her fingers and wondered what was happening, she stopped.

"Don't stop," Logan cried.

Taryn began again, but this time her lips kissed down Logan until they got to the nub and licked, just as she remembered Logan doing. Logan's movements intensified, and Taryn had to hold on to the rocking hips. To her surprise, she could feel pleasure mounting again between her own legs. Never had she felts such intensity from her body.

Logan's body suddenly stopped and she cried out, "God, yes," before one last shattering movement.

Logan opened her eyes and smiled, noticing the sun streaming through the small window. The night before had been incredible. Taryn made her feel more than she thought

117

she could ever feel again. They'd made love several times, before exhaustion finally overtook them.

"Good morning." Taryn snuggled even closer, if that was possible in the narrow bed.

"Good morning." Logan smiled and kissed her lover.

"Thank you."

"I'm the one who should be thanking you, Taryn." Logan sat up. "Be right back, I need to go to the bathroom." When she returned to the room, Taryn was sitting up with a worried look on her face. "What's wrong?" Logan asked

"I think I started my period." She motioned to the blood on the sheet.

Logan took a few steps before engulfing Taryn in her arms. "No, you haven't. It is not uncommon to bleed your first time," she said softly.

A relieved look crossed Taryn's face, before she grinned and pulled back the sheet fully. "In that case, would you care to join me?"

"You betcha." Logan kissed Taryn passionately, as she slipped into the crumpled bed linen.

†

"Do you think we can use your mom's car again, or shall we just mosey around town?" Logan asked, as she watched Taryn slip into a skimpy T-shirt that left nothing to the imagination. "I like." She wiggled her eyebrows while staring at Taryn's breasts and licking her lips.

"If she's in a good mood maybe, but don't hold your breath."

Logan stretched, as she contemplated the chance of Brenda being in a good mood. *Maybe she had a good poker night. We can live in hope.* "Let's find out, shall we? I heard footsteps down the hall when you were in the bathroom."

"Okay, I'll be right behind you. I just need to finish dressing."

Logan grinned. "I don't know. I kind of like you with just that T-shirt on." She gave a wink left the room. Closing the door, she heard Taryn giggle. This was turning out to be one hell of a great, unexpected, long weekend.

Moments later, she stood in the doorway of the kitchen and saw Brenda seated at the table, a mug of coffee in one hand and the newspaper in the other. "Morning, Brenda."

"Well, look at who finally got up…the dyke who did my daughter last night."

Logan sucked in a deep breath. *I can do this, I really can. Be nice. Be nice.* "How was the poker game?" She entered the room and stood opposite the woman.

"None of your business. When are you leaving?" Brenda snarled before slamming her hand on the table. "I'm the one who will have to listen to her bellyaching when you leave. I'm the one who will have to live with the shame of having a queer daughter." She snarled her lips. "Get the hell out of my house."

"I'm leaving in the morning when I get my vehicle that should be fixed by then." Logan scratched the side of her neck. "There isn't any shame in being a lesbian these days. Unless you are narrow minded, but then, I guess this town might be to some…. They haven't treated you so well, have they? Don't they call you the town whore?" She closed her eyes and wished the last words unsaid. *Crap, this isn't going well.*

Brenda slammed both hands on the table and stood, her face red with rage. "How dare you talk to me in that manner. I'll have you know that I am a God-fearing, church-going woman. I may have gentlemen callers, but I'm not a perverted bitch like you."

Taryn walked into the kitchen. "Hey, what's going on? I bet the neighbors can hear you." She looked at Logan. "You are my guest, so don't let her speak to you that way."

"Another perverted voice. How does it feel to be her bitch? You're just another conquest to her. She'll be leaving you behind tomorrow, how you gonna feel about that?"

Logan stared at Brenda wanting to throttle her for being such a nasty woman toward her daughter. *How do people get that way? Taryn is such a sweet person.*

"Brenda, there is only one bitch in this house, and it isn't me or Logan. Maybe you should take a good look in the mirror sometime and see what everyone else does," Taryn calmly said.

Wow, when did she become so brave? Logan's heart swelled in pride for her lover.

"I will not allow you to speak to me in that manner. I am your mother, and you owe me respect."

"You certainly don't act like a mother."

"Enough. This is *my* house, and I will not tolerate your back talk."

Taryn sneered. "No problem." She plucked the car keys off the hook. "What do you say we go to Sanderson Cross and try out that little diner we saw?"

"No. You can't take my car."

"Yes, I can, Brenda. Remember, Logan paid you for the room and the use of the car. So unless you want to pony up the hundred dollars, we are out of here."

Logan heard spluttering noises from Brenda and saw an astonished look on her face. "I guess the decision is made, and I'm leaving with Taryn." She smiled at Taryn who was clinking the keys in her hands then turned back to Brenda. "Oh, I'll be back later."

Taryn took her hand, and they left the house.

As they approached the car, Logan pulled Taryn close. "I am so damn proud of you." She gently kissed Taryn, who nestled close to her chest at the touch.

Brenda came charging out on to the porch. "I'll call the sheriff on you if you touch my car."

"Go ahead, Brenda. Of course, if you do, I may have to go around to all the wives in town and tell them you're sleeping with their husbands."

"You wouldn't dare."

Taryn grinned. "I would. So, if I see any sign of a police car after me—" She shrugged. "—well it won't be pretty for you."

Brenda opened her mouth then shut it. "When did you grow a pair?"

"Always had them, just didn't realize it. Don't wait up for us." Taryn gave her a little wave before giving the keys to Logan and getting in on the passenger's side.

Logan climbed into the car. "You do know that letting me drive will piss your mother off even more."

Taryn grinned. "Yeah, isn't it great? Now, let's get that motor running."

"At your command." Logan twisted the key in the ignition, and the engine roared to life. Seconds later, they sped away from the house.

Taryn scooted over and sat next to Logan before running her hand along her leg. "Have you ever done it in the backseat of a car?"

Logan nodded.

"I am so turned on right now that the backseat is looking very inviting."

"You certainly have got a tiger in the tank this morning. How about we head for the parking lot near the river, if you can wait that long?" Logan could feel the wetness beginning between her legs. Taryn was turning out to be unexpected in a very sexy way, and she wasn't going to miss out on any of it.

"I have a better place. My grandparents' old homestead. There's a really great hay loft there, and we can park the car inside the barn, just in case she does call the sheriff."

"Direct me. I'm all for a romp in the hayloft. It will be a first for me." Logan smiled. *Who would have thought I'd have a first in this town?*

†

The convertible came to a stop in front of a somewhat dilapidated old house, and Taryn rested her arms on Logan's shoulder. "Well, this is it." She let out a sigh. "My fondest memories are all in there. I sometimes wish I could restore her and live here."

Logan could hear the sadness behind Taryn's words and put her arm around her shoulder and pulled her close. "Will you show me?"

"The last time I came here was five years ago, and it wasn't in very good shape then. I'm afraid you might fall through one of the floor boards."

"I'll take my chances." Logan opened the car door and got out and went around to open Taryn's door. "Come on, it'll be fun."

"But, I thought we were going to check out the barn. It's in much better shape…I think."

As Taryn stepped out of the car, Logan cupped her lover's chin gently in her hands and stared into her eyes. "Somehow, I think coming here has doused that passion you had. Let's look down memory lane, shall we? Sometimes we need to do that to move on." She relinquished her hold and stepped back, allowing Taryn space.

"I'm sorry for being such a downer."

"Never be sorry…unless of course you cheat on me. Then be very, very sorry." Logan grinned and wriggled her eyebrows.

"You'd care if I cheated on you? Really?" She laughed. "Have you seen the pickin's in Bourne Falls?"

Logan chuckled. "Okay, point taken. Now, show me this place that you have so many good memories of. I'm fascinated." She took Taryn's hand, as they moved toward the house.

"I'd be glad to. Come on." They walked up rickety steps and opened the front door. "I remember it to be much different than it is now," she said wistfully. "My granny was a stickler for cleanliness." She pushed open the door wider. "Be careful, the floor boards are shaky at best."

Logan released Taryn's hand and tentatively stepped inside the building. "One of the reasons I love traveling around is because of old buildings like these. I've got an old digital camera, when I say old, it's about ten years, but it still takes fantastic pictures. Anyway, I love taking shots of these types of buildings and musing about who lived in them and the stories they could tell." A puff of dust engulfed her boot, as she walked deeper into the interior. A wooden table with only three legs was standing precariously upright. The touch of a hand on the surface would probably topple it completely. "Hey, one thing this time around is that I'm going to hear some of those stories, right?"

"Yes." Taryn went around in a circle then stopped when a mouse scampered past her. "This was the room I spent the most time in. Pops would sit in his chair over the by the fireplace and tell me all kinds of stories about my dad growing up. I loved hearing them, because they brought him to life for me." She walked toward a door and swung it open.

"In here was the kitchen. I spent a lot of time in here with my granny." Taryn smiled. "She told me all her secret recipes."

Logan looked over the small, square kitchen. The cupboards on the wall were mainly intact, except for two doors hanging from their hinges. She moved forward and touched the light oak surface. In the city, someone would pay a fortune for them, even in their present condition. She turned and watched Taryn's wistful expression. "You know, from what I can see the house is in pretty good shape. It would take work, but it can definitely be saved."

"If I had the money, I'd fix it up and live here."

"Perhaps, one day you will." Logan smiled. "The memories we have of our youth are often the happiest. I remember my gran taking me back to where she grew up. The Oneida Nation, in Wisconsin, was an awesome place, and I can still remember the joy in her face when she told me about living there."

"From what you've told me about her, she sounds like a wonderful person." Taryn walked over to the porcelain-enameled, cast-iron sink and ran her finger over a dark scar on its surface. "This happened when Pops surprised Granny, and she dropped a heavy skillet in the sink." She laughed. "I can still hear her screaming." She let out a long sigh. "How did I let my life get so far away from who I was here?"

Logan frowned, then moved to Taryn's side and engulfed her in a hug. "Hey, life throws us curve balls that we can't avoid, no matter how much we duck. Don't write yourself off. You are way too young for that. To be honest, I've always thought that if you want something badly enough it will happen, but you have to be willing to work hard for it. I think you took the first steps this weekend, with Brenda."

Taryn smiled and lifted one shoulder. "Yeah, you're right. I did, didn't I?" She took Logan's hand and pulled her close. "In less than twenty-four hours, you will be on your way, so I'm not going to waste any more time on what could have been. What do you say we go check out the barn? Did you see the windmill or the silo when we drove up?"

Logan laughed, then bent her head and snatched a kiss. "I sure did. I love those old windmills. Let's go explore more, and you can tell me another story."

†

"Wow. This is fantastic." Logan's eyes ran over the old, weathered barn. "Do you know people pay top dollar for barn wood? I've seen a show on TV where they actually rejuvenate barns."

Taryn took her hand and pulled her toward the barn door. "Come on, let's go inside. It hasn't been as ruined as the house."

Inside, Logan couldn't believe her eyes. "Is this the way you remember it as a kid?"

"Pretty much."

Logan pulled Taryn to her and held her tight. "Tell me about them."

"My grandparents?"

"Yes."

Taryn took a step back. "Five months after we moved to town, my other grandmother, who we lived with, died. I think Brenda was anxious to get rid of me after that, because she always sent me out here to spend the summer." A winsome smile crossed her face. "I looked forward to spending the summers here. Unlike Brenda, they actually cared about me. I learned so much from them. I watched Pops making a wind chime for Granny and asked him to teach me. Everything I know about metal art, I learned from him."

"He must have been a great teacher, if what I've seen you create is anything to go by."

Taryn nodded. "He died when I was seventeen, and Granny died six months later. I'd spent that summer with her, and I could tell that her heart was broken." She blew out a breath and brushed a tear away. "I miss them terribly."

Logan went to Taryn and hugged her close. "Go ahead and cry. I've got you."

Taryn looked up at her, then pressed lips to her cheek, kissing her way to waiting lips. "Make love to me," she whispered before snaking her hand under Logan's shirt.

Logan knew that Taryn was at her most vulnerable, and the tender feelings that bubbled in her heart overwhelmed her. Never had any of her lovers made her feel like anything more than a means to an end. Yet, here she was completely open, wanting to give all of herself to Taryn. Logan lifted her and carried her over to a pile of hay before laying her down gently. "Gladly." She wanted to show Taryn all the deep emotions she was feeling and began to undress her, kissing every part she exposed. Her fingers ran over a hardened nipple before squeezing it. "Do you like that?"

"Oh, yes."

Logan left no part of Taryn's body untouched. She reveled in the way Taryn reacted to her touch, moaning as her passion rose. "You're so beautiful." Her tongue ran over the pulsating clit, while her fingers slowly entered her. To her surprise, her body was soon on the edge of climax, and when Taryn cried out in pleasure, Logan felt herself go over the edge too.

Taryn snuggled next to her and kissed her cheek. "Now I have another wonderful memory of this place."

"As do I." Logan rolled over on top of Taryn, and their loving began again.

Later, Logan looked at Taryn and smiled. "I'm not much of an expert, but isn't this hay fresh? I would have thought it'd be…I don't know…moldy."

Taryn sat up and looked around. "That's strange." Her eyes widened. "I bet Brenda let one of her men friends store their hay in here." She snorted. "Probably charged him for it."

Logan laughed and pulled Taryn to her before kissing her soundly.

CHAPTER TEN

It was past noon when they finally left the farm, sated and happy. During the drive to Sanderson Cross, Taryn sat as close to Logan as she could, while resting her hand on her thigh. She was still basking in the glow of their lovemaking, when her stomach growled loudly. "Yikes, I think it's telling me I haven't had enough to eat." She winked at Logan. "Well, food anyway."

"Hmm, so you've done with me now that you had me." Logan grinned. "There was that small coffee shop that sold food in the mall. We only tried the coffee last time. Let's go there. I want to check out the competition."

"Great idea. Do you remember how to get there?"

"I know where it is. I have a good memory for places I've been to before. My mom used to say I'd never get lost, even in a dense forest, if I'd been taken there once before." Logan smiled. "She was right of course." She steered the car left at the light, and the mall came to view. "See what I mean?"

When they entered the café, Taryn took in the intimate feel of the place. She pursued the menu noting that it also reflected the ambiance. Featured on the menu were all kinds of gourmet salads, sandwiches, and wraps. "What are you hungry for?" Taryn asked. "I think I'll get that salad with fresh strawberries and blueberries."

"Hmm, the chicken Cesar wrap looks good. Want any fries or onion rings?"

Taryn smiled. She loved it when Logan looked at her. "I see they have truffle fries. I've never heard of that before. Do you know what they are?"

Logan stroked her chin. "Nope. Let's be decadent and try them."

The server, a young man who hardly looked old enough to be out of high school, arrived at that moment. He had pimples everywhere and a sullen expression. "What can I get you?" His pen was poised over the pad he held, as his eyes darted over to a table where several girls were laughing and joking around.

"Exactly what are truffle fries?" Taryn asked.

"Hey, I don't know. Ask the cook. All I know is that everyone seems to like them."

"Thanks," Taryn said sarcastically. "I'll have the salad with fresh fruit."

"Dressing?"

"Balsamic vinaigrette."

"And, you?" He looked at Logan.

"I'll have the Cesar wrap."

The server wandered off toward the table with the young girls and stopped to talk to them.

"Don't think we'll be getting our order quickly, do you?" Logan shrugged.

"By the looks of that guy, I doubt it. I know we'd never stand for that kind of thing at the Tavern."

Logan placed the menu back in the holder. "How is Rosie? I like her. She was genuinely friendly. In fact, to be honest, the only person who has really taken any umbrage with me and my lifestyle is your mother. Bourne Falls isn't so bad. Believe me on that front. I have a multitude of friends who would live here in a shot if they thought it was so tolerant."

Taryn shook her head and looked away. "Rosie is my only friend in town, and she's leaving."

"Why?"

"Rosie got a chance to leave that hell hole of a town and took it. She's going to Florida to live with her sister who recently lost her husband."

"Well, good for her. She'll love Florida, and they do say it's a great place to find a husband. Lots of rich, old men." Logan chuckled.

"I don't think she'll go down that road. From what she's said, her marriage to Bill Bickerson was worse than his name."

Logan shook her head. "Well, if he's a rich, old man, at least she can have loads of money to spend in her misery. So, when does she leave?"

"End of the week. I'll miss her almost as much as I'll miss you when you leave tomorrow." She watched Logan purse her lips then give her a focused look.

"If I could stay I would. No, let's be honest. I wouldn't stay here. It really doesn't suit me, at least not Bourne Falls. I'm serious about the business we saw here in Sanderson. Not sure about the logistics of it all of course, but it might work out." She reached across the table and took Taryn's hands in hers. "We can keep in touch."

"We can? Just how do you think that will happen?" Taryn pulled her hand away. "Will you call me where I live? Brenda won't allow that. Or, maybe you'll call me at work. That'll go over big." She took Logan's hand. "I'm sorry, I was out of line. It's just, you've come into my life and shown me how wonderful life can be." She brushed away a tear. "Once you're gone, I'll go back to Taryn the loser. At least for a while, I was so much more, thanks to you."

"Hey, Taryn, don't cry. You're not a loser. I wouldn't like you or even be your lover if you were. I'll make it my mission in life to keep in touch. Okay?" Logan pulled her hands away and rummaged in her pocket. "Take this."

"A phone?"

"Yep. I bought this one to travel with. I have my iPhone at home. I wasn't going to take the chance of losing it on a trip, so bought this pay-as-you-go Android." Logan smiled.

"For me?" Taryn saw Logan nod. "Oh, Logan, this is the best gift anyone has ever given me. How do I use it? How much will it cost me?"

"At the moment, nothing. I think there is still fifty dollars on there. After that, you simply go to a store and pick up a top-up card. It works like a normal phone, and it does have apps as well." Logan looked around. "Just give me a minute, okay?"

Taryn, fascinated with her new phone, almost missed Logan having words with the boy who was still talking with the girls. She watched, as he scurried away with a deep scowl. Logan strode back, and Taryn's heart almost missed a beat. "Want to go elsewhere?"

Logan sat and narrowed her eyes. "Nope, we are going to have those truffle fries, even if I have to cook them myself. Here, let me show you how it works."

†

Logan grinned, as Taryn asked her for the tenth time where she was taking her. "It wouldn't be a surprise if I told you, now would it? We're nearly there." She watched

Taryn's head switch from side to side, as they passed several shops in the mall.

"Oh, come on, Logan, I hate surprises."

Logan waved her finger at Taryn and winked. "You will like this surprise. Just around the corner." Logan took her hand and almost frog marched her around the corner to a low building that had three shops.

"Shopping? That's my surprise?"

Logan laughed and pulled her toward the middle shop in the row. "Step inside." She opened the door, and Taryn frowned but did as asked. As they walked inside, a bell rang out above their head. A middle-aged man poked his head around the door at the back and smiled.

"Be right with you."

"Mind if we browse?" Logan said.

"Go ahead. Shout out if you need anything." He disappeared behind the door and the sound of a machine could be heard in the background.

"What do you think? Are you surprised?"

"This is amazing. I wish I could do work like this." Taryn frowned. "When did you find this place?"

"Well, when you went to the bathroom across the street, I saw it by accident. We didn't have the time to go inside then, so I figured today was a great day to show you. You do know what this means?" Logan fingered a delicate piece of metal turned into a butterfly.

"Um, that there's a market for my metal work." Taryn picked up a small daisy painted a bright yellow with a brown center. "I've never done anything so small before. I wonder how he does it."

Logan considered that. "Let's ask the guy." She smiled. "If you're available, we have some questions," she shouted out to the partially open door.

132

A minute later, the sandy-haired man entered the room wiping his hands on a rag. "What can I do for you both?"

Logan watched the smile that ventured over the man's lips and the twinkle in his eyes. *He looks like a nice fellow.* "These pieces are amazing. My friend here works in metal, and she was wondering how you do these, being so small and all."

"Ah, well, it's a bit like working with fine jewelry. If you have the skills, it isn't difficult to train yourself to do this style too." He turned to Taryn.

"Where would I get that kind of training?"

The man scratched the day-old stubble on his chin and grinned. "You're looking at him. I teach a class at the local high school once a month, if you're interested?" He rummaged around on his desk and held out a flyer. "Here you go. It has all the details."

"Um, thanks. I don't know if I can get there. I live in Bourne Falls and have to rely on someone to drive me or borrow a car."

Logan pursed her lips at the solemn statement. *Damn Brenda and her intractable views regarding her daughter.* "Sorry I can't help on that one, love," she whispered to Taryn. "Do you have any books or material that might help?"

"Sure, we do. Come this way." He motioned for them to follow, but Logan held back as Taryn went to check out the books on the far wall.

She wandered around the tables of displays and then gazed at larger pieces on the wall similar in size to Taryn's work. Her lover's pieces were so much better, at least to her eye.

"You won't be taking up the metalcraft?" the man called across to her.

"Oh, no. Taryn has all the talent in that department." She meandered over to them and saw Taryn drop her head. "Don't you?"

"My grandad taught me all about metal work."

"What's his name?" the man asked.

"Was. His name was Ben...Ben Donovan."

"Well, I'll be darned. I remember him. He and my dad were friends."

Taryn looked bewildered. "He was a great guy."

Logan figured Taryn was out of her element by her shy reply. Most would have been more excited at the prospect of someone knowing their kin and would want to know more. "They were friends because of the metalworking or something else?"

"First, I apologize. My name is Ken Stuart. My dad was Alvin. He hated the name and would only reply to Al." Ken chuckled. "Great guy, my dad. He and Ben used to go to school together and even went in the army at the same time. I think they lost touch when my dad went to live in California for a while."

Logan grinned. "Taryn, now you know a little more about your grandad. Isn't that great? I call it a small world. You never know who you are going to meet that will change your life."

Taryn smiled. "Yes, it is. Mr. Stuart, would it be okay if one day I brought in some of my work? I'd like to know what you think."

"Of course, for a pal of my dad's, anything. Incidentally, if you give me enough notice, I can have my dad here. I'm sure he would love to meet the granddaughter of his old friend. My number is on the flyer."

"Um, thanks." Taryn looked away and began fingering a metal seagull. She looked at Logan and smiled. "I have a phone now, so I can call you when I want." A blush colored her cheeks.

"Wonderful. If you really are interested in making the small stuff, you should get a copy of this." He pointed to a large, hardback volume.

"Wow, that's enormous. It's bigger than my coffee table at home." Logan laughed, as she looked at the book and flicked over several pages which had marvelous glossy photos along with the writing. "What do you think of this, Taryn? It looks great to me."

Taryn scratched her ear and looked at the book. "I'd have to save up to afford something like that, Logan," she whispered. "It is beautiful though."

"Okay, a birthday present or Christmas maybe," Logan said and then flicked a look at the man at their side. "Anything a bit less showy?"

Ken nodded and picked up a nondescript looking paperback. "This was my first book when I began. A bit dated regarding the equipment, but the practices still hold true today." He handed it to Taryn.

As she turned the pages, Taryn's eyes gazed at what was there. "This is fantastic. Everything has so much detail for me about how to work the metal." She handed the book back to the man. "How much is it please?"

"For you, ten dollars."

Taryn sucked in a breath. "Okay, I can do that."

"Great, want to look at anything else?"

Logan smiled slowly, as she watched Taryn's interaction with the man, especially when it came to buying the book. "I was just wondering if these are all your own work, or do you sell commission pieces?"

"Good question. Mostly mine, but occasionally, if someone is really good, I let them sell out of this place for a small fee. To be honest, not that I like people to know, I just love creating things. The hard sell isn't my style, much to my wife's disappointment." He laughed, as he headed for the counter and began placing the book in a paper bag.

Logan turned to Taryn and whispered, "Who knows, maybe your work will be displayed here one day."

Taryn let out a derisive sound. "Yeah, right."

Logan chuckled, as she paid the man. With cheery goodbyes and "see you soon," they left the shop. "What did you think of my surprise?"

"I loved it. You didn't need to buy that book for me." She dug in her pocket and pulled out a bunch of ones and began counting them. "Did he charge you tax?"

"You are joking, right? It was only ten dollars. Besides, it was my surprise to you, so no more mention of paying me back. Right. Where to now? Don't forget, I still have to check on Shelia."

"Well, knowing Tommy, I'd say we should get there as soon as possible. He tends to just leave when he feels like it."

"Sounds good to me. Can I drive?"

†

The red convertible pulled up in front of Bourne Falls Garage and Logan got out. "I'll be right back, as soon as I check on Shelia."

"Good luck," Taryn said. "Don't let Tommy bamboozle you."

"Won't happen."

Taryn watched the sway of Logan's hips as she approached the garage. "Please, please don't let it be ready." Logan had given her life, and she didn't want to lose it just yet. Her heart sank ten minutes later, when she saw a truck with an out-of-state license plate back out of the garage. The

136

Ranger pulled up next to her, and a beaming Logan leaned across the seat before winding down the window.

"Shelia is all better. I'll follow you to the house."

"Okay," Taryn said, trying hard to keep the disappointment from her voice. It was only two o'clock, giving Logan plenty of time to leave for St. Louis.

The two cars pulled up in front of the run-down house that Taryn called home. She got out of the car after raising the roof, picked up her book, and dragged her feet toward Logan.

"Isn't she beautiful?" Logan enthused. "And, she's running like she's brand new."

"A day early too. That must be some kind of record for Tommy. I've heard he isn't all that reliable." She held up the book. "Thank you for the book."

Logan grinned. "I guess I scared him." She put her arm around Taryn's shoulder. "I hope you can learn a lot from the book and make me something special."

"I'll do that." Taryn kicked the ground, not wanting to say goodbye.

"What do you want to do next? Go for a spin in Shelia?"

Taryn's eyes widened. "You aren't leaving now?"

"Not unless you want me to." Her eyebrows knitted. "I thought we had one more night together."

"We do. I just thought you might want to get started back on your journey."

"Hmm, let me think." She put a finger to her cheek. "I can get in Shelia and make a long, lonely drive or…I could spend the rest of the day and night with a gorgeous woman who makes me all hot and bothered." She winked. "That is a tough choice."

"Logan, stop teasing me. I want you to stay with me for as long as you can." She took a step and pulled Logan to her and kissed her.

Brenda came flying out of the house. "Finally, my car is back." She glared at Logan. "See you got your truck, so I guess you'll be leavin' now."

Taryn stepped in front of Logan. "The deal that she paid you for was for tonight and the use of your car."

"You can't have my car. Besides you got hers now."

"Then give her some of her money back."

Logan placed a hand on Taryn's shoulder. "Let her have it. We don't need her car anymore."

Taryn turned and gave Logan a passionate kiss that went on and on. When they broke apart, she whispered, "That'll drive her crazy."

As if on cue, Brenda said, "Degenerates. You're throwin' away your reputation for that dyke. People are already talkin' about you two."

"Let them talk, Brenda, I don't care." She looked at Logan. "What do you say we get out of here and you can show Shelia off."

"Sounds good to me. Shall we take a blanket, a bottle of wine, and a picnic basket?"

"I'll get the blanket, and we can stop at the Quick Mart for the rest." Taryn leaned into Logan and kissed her again, before running into the house.

"She just wanted you for a quick roll in the hay. You'll never see her again," Brenda screamed as Taryn ran by.

"You'd know all about that, Brenda."

With ease, Logan stepped out of her truck and sauntered over to Brenda.

"What do you want?"

The sneer that went with the question wasn't a surprise. Surely, somewhere in the woman, there was compassion for her daughter. "Did you want children, Brenda?"

Brenda scowled. "What's it to you? That's my business."

"Just wondering, as you aren't that nice to your only child. I would have thought you'd love her more after your husband passed." Logan leaned against the faded paint of the post leading to the porch.

"I'll have you know that I was the belle of this town in my day. JR promised me, when we got hitched, that he'd take me out of this godforsaken place."

"Why didn't he?" Logan stared at Brenda and saw a faraway look in her eyes. Then her features turned to stone.

"I fell pregnant, end of that dream. So, in answer to your question, no. I never wanted children, and now, even more so. No chance of her finding a decent man who can give us both a better life. You spoiled her for that."

Logan's heart flipped. Taryn's head appeared slowly through the doorjamb, her complexion pale, her expression…desolate. *Damn, no one needs to find out that they aren't wanted like that.* "Hey, got that blanket?"

Taryn nodded. Without a glance at Brenda, she ran toward the truck.

"See, she doesn't have the manners to say goodbye." Brenda waved her hand in the air and entered the house, slamming the door behind her.

Logan waited a second or two and took a deep breath. She turned and made her way back to Taryn, now seated in the passenger side of the truck. Opening the door, she gave her a sheepish look. "You heard that, didn't you?"

"Yes." The word was said through gritted teeth. "Not that I'm surprised. I always thought she hated me."

Logan dragged herself into the driver's seat and frowned. "Some people aren't meant to be parents."

"Sure. Let's go, I need that glass of wine right now."

Logan nodded and started the truck. She glanced at Taryn's bowed head and saw her flick a hand toward her eyes. *Damn, I wish I'd never talked to Brenda now.* She engaged the gear and set off down the street.

CHAPTER ELEVEN

"Where shall we go for our picnic?" Logan slowly drew the truck to a stop outside the mini-mart.

Taryn pursed her lips and stroked her chin.

"Hmm, have you seen the town park? It's beautiful right now, with all the roses blooming." She eyed Logan and shrugged. "It's about the only place decent in this town. Franny Grant has made it her mission to keep the park in pristine condition. If only everyone else was that dedicated."

"It would make a big difference in the town, that's for sure." Logan began to climb out of the truck. "I went there on the first day, but I'm happy to go back. I thought it was a lovely, restful place."

"Yeah, I agree. When I have a big fall out with Brenda, I go there to think. Some of my best inspiration comes from a visit to that area."

Logan chuckled. "Then it's a must. Let's find out what this place has in the way of wine. Shall we?" Ten minutes later they were back in the truck.

"God, can you believe it? No wine. Thank goodness, there was at least a six-pack of beer." Taryn muttered.

"Beer works. Besides, wine goes to my head, and I'm driving, so it might be one of those blessings in disguise." Logan drove away toward the park. The ornate bandstand stood out, as she parked opposite it. "Time for your inspiration session."

Taryn was carrying the blanket, and Logan followed her to a shady area under a large oak tree located at the back of the park. Taryn spread the blanket out. "I like this place, because it is as far away as possible from the road. No one ever bothers to come way out here." She took Logan's hand. "Let's sit and enjoy our picnic."

Logan reached into the brown paper bag and withdrew the beer. "We're going to have to drink out of the bottle. I hope that's okay." She inspected the cap and saw it wasn't a twist off. "Need a bottle opener, but I have my trusty, all-purpose gadget on my belt." She unhooked a Swiss army knife from her belt and proceeded to open the two bottles before passing one to Taryn.

Taryn took a long pull from the bottle then put it down. "You know, I've never been here with anyone." She smiled. "It's nice to not be alone. Thank you for coming into my life, Logan."

Logan smiled and tipped her bottle against the neck of Taryn's. "Thank you for making this trip even more special than I could have ever have imagined it would be. This might sound corny, but I'll never forget this experience, as long as I live."

"Me too." Taryn looked up at the tree and waved her hand. "Every time I leave here, I go back to my welding and try to recreate what I see when I look up there." She shook her head. "I can never quite capture what I see."

Logan looked up at the tree. "Okay, tell me what you see."

"This will sound strange, but I see the tree of life. All the branches going in every direction yet bound to one another." She sighed. "That is what I think family should be."

"Hmm." Logan lay down on the blanket and looked up at the tree. It was a mass of branches with bright-green leaves, but otherwise nothing spectacular to her. She pulled Taryn down to lay beside her. "Point out to me where you see this, because I have to admit my brain doesn't compute it."

Taryn lifted her arm and pointed at a long, gnarly branch. "Do you see that branch there...the weirdly shaped one?"

"Yes."

"That is the grandfather, and that one that is a bit smaller is the grandmother. All the little branches are the children and grandchildren. You know they're kids, because they're dancing wildly in the breeze. If you follow that group, you will see they are all linked to the trunk, as are all the rest of the branches on the tree."

"Wow, I can see that now you've described it to me. The tree of life...I've never thought of it like that, but now I'll always see trees that way. I think it's a great analogy. Thank you for sharing your creativity." Logan leaned up on her elbow and stared into Taryn's eyes. "That new book and maybe lessons will help you create exactly what you see there. Can't wait for you to show that to me one day."

"You'll be around then?" There was a tentative sound to Taryn's voice. She sat up and began rummaging in the other bag before pulling out two foil-wrapped items. "Shall we see what the mini-mart's burritos taste like?" She grinned. "If I wasn't so hungry, I'd be very afraid. Okay, I am afraid, but hungry."

"Yeah, me too. Those truffle fries were good, but the portions were miniscule. Definitely room for another café there, in my humble opinion." Logan took the burrito and opened the package, sniffing the food before she bit into it. "Tastes pretty good, actually," she said once she'd swallowed the portion.

Taryn took a tentative bite and smiled. "I'll have to remember to check that place out more often."

"The phone I gave you takes pictures. Remember, we took some at the viewing platform yesterday. Maybe you will send me pictures of what you're working on. Does that sound like a plan?" Logan continued to consume the burrito but watched Taryn's face. *She really is very expressive without words.*

"Sure, I can do that if you show me how." She lifted a shoulder. "I never could afford a phone. Once, I asked Brenda if she'd get me one for my birthday." Taryn laughed bitterly. "My birthday came and went without a word from her. I guess I should have realized then she wanted nothing to do with me. But, I reasoned that she was my mother, and I wanted to think the best, even though I knew it wasn't going to happen." Taryn smiled. "Enough of this, tell me about where you are going and what you'll be doing."

Logan gave a sympathetic smile. "Actually, I'm going home tomorrow. I was due to go to St. Louis as my final destination, but being here with you…well to be honest, I don't think it could compare." She touched a light finger to Taryn's red stained cheeks. "I need to check on my folks. They were hassling me to visit before I found another job. So, maybe I will venture there for a week or so. Otherwise, it's job hunting time for me."

"What kind of job? I know you liked that café we looked at. Is that what you really want to do? Own a restaurant or be a chef?"

Logan shook her head. "I'm more a creative barista than a chef. As I said before, I was trained very well by my ex. For sure, I want to pursue something along those lines. I have to say that place was in my price range and looked like a great opportunity."

"Do you still have contact with your ex?"

Logan gave Taryn a long stare, then she leaned back on her hands and sighed. "Hardly. That woman did the dirty on me, big time. I'm afraid I don't forgive cheating."

Taryn suddenly moved on top of her chest and dragged the blanket around them before depositing feather-light kisses all over Logan's face. The kisses travelled down to her neck and to the hollow of her breasts. Sucking in a deep breath as her body responded to Taryn's touch, Logan snaked a hand and unbuttoned Taryn's jeans. She began an erotic exploration of her own.

Taryn sat resting her head on Logan's shoulder, sated for the moment. She laughed. "I can't believe I did that to you here in the park."

Logan kissed the top of her head. "It's a first for me and a very pleasurable one, I have to say. Never made love in a park before, and I loved every second of it. You are really making it difficult for me to leave Bourne Falls. Who would have believed it, right?"

"I have to admit I don't want to see you go, Logan." Taryn looked away, not wanting Logan to see the distress she felt. "I have never known anyone like you." She turned back and smiled. "You came into my life, and everything has changed for me. I have a backbone now, when I never did, and some people even know I exist. I will be eternally grateful to you for that."

Logan turned Taryn's face to hers. "You always had a backbone, Taryn. You are a lovely, spirited, young woman who has had a hard life with people who should have loved you unconditionally and didn't. I find that so hard to understand. I believe in my heart—" Logan touched a finger to her chest. "—that you are going to succeed out of all proportion to what you know now. I'm going to be so proud to be a part of that."

"That is exactly why you are so good for me. I don't know if the person you think I am will be able to shine through once you're gone." She bit her lip. "I guess what I'm trying to say is…don't let go."

Logan dropped her gaze.

Taryn didn't know what to make of Logan not looking at her. "I've said too much and put you in an awkward position, haven't I? I'm so sorry." She could hear the tremble in her voice but carried on. "Will you forgive me? Please."

"Hey, nothing to forgive. I feel like a heel. I've spent a great three days with you. You've given me everything without any strings, and all I can say at this moment is that *yes* tomorrow I have to leave."

"I gladly gave to you, Logan. And, don't forget, I did take from you when you taught me how to love you and please you." She smiled. "I will never forget you for as long as I live."

"I want to say that what we have will last forever, Taryn. But this is your first experience loving another woman, and I've been burned badly in the past. As much as I hate to say this, I want to get to know you better before I say it's forever. For the near future that's gonna have to be from a distance. Is that cool with you?"

"Yes, so let's not waste the time we have left. We went to the falls, now I'll take you to Look Out Point. It's a great place to watch the sun go down."

"Was that the place we went to yesterday?"

"No. This is ten times better, and the view is spectacular. If we time it right, we may even see bats coming out of a nearby cave." Taryn grinned. "Are you game?"

Logan placed her arms around Taryn's shoulders and drew her close. "You are a marvel." She kissed her soundly.

"Come on, let's go. We can sit in your truck and make out while we wait for the sun to go down." She wiggled her eyebrows. "Or me."

†

The old, wooden floorboards creaked, as they walked the few steps to the door of Taryn's home. Logan silently hoped Brenda wasn't there, for she'd had enough confrontations with the woman to last her a lifetime. Thing was, if Taryn remained in her life, Brenda was part of it, no matter what. *Darn that old saying. You can choose your friends but not your relatives.*

"If she has a new boyfriend, she won't be home, if that's what's making you scowl," Taryn said with a wink.

Logan shrugged. "Wow, you know me so well and in such a short space of time." She gave a tight smile. "I just didn't want to have another battle with your mother."

"There was a time when I cared what she thought, but after these last few days with you, I realize that I've let her control me for way too long." Taryn put her hand on the doorknob. "Even if she's here, we can just go straight to my room."

Logan nodded. "Yeah, I think that's for the best."

They entered the house and immediately heard a television blaring. "Guess no new boyfriend in tow," she whispered, and Taryn turned to her and rolled her eyes. A part of Logan wanted to run to Taryn's room and escape the wrath of the woman, but the better part of her wanted to at least say goodbye. It was the right thing to do. Instead of following Taryn down the hall, she walked toward the sound of the TV.

"Where are you going?" Taryn whispered.

"To say goodbye to your mother." Logan entered the room.

"Well, well look who the slutty cat drug in again. Are you going to do the nasty to my daughter again?"

"Brenda, stop! Logan is a guest, so treat her just like you do all your men friends that spend the night."

Brenda rose from her chair and walked over to stand in front of Taryn. "How dare you speak to me in that tone." Her hand connected with Taryn's cheek. "Get that woman out of my house. Now."

Logan moved like lightening, but couldn't stop the assault before the audible crack of a hand hitting flesh rung out in the room. "For god's sake, why did you do that? She's your only child." Logan placed herself between the two women and gave Taryn a tender look, as she placed a finger on the glowing cheek. "Are you okay?"

"Yeah, it's not like that's the first time. Come on, let's go to my room."

"No, Taryn, not yet." She gave Taryn a smile. "You go, and I'll catch up with you. I promise this will only take a few minutes."

Taryn shook her head and left the room, her hand smoothing down the skin of her red cheek.

Logan, crossing her arms over her chest, turned to the older woman. "So, Brenda, do you want to slap me too?"

Brenda picked up a glass and took a long swallow of beer. "Girly, you better hope I don't, 'cause when I start on you you'll beg me to stop." She put her glass down and walked so she was in Logan's space. "Get the hell out of my house and stop corrupting her."

Logan's stomach tightened at the obnoxious behavior of this human being, and that was the best she would ever call Brenda. She certainly wasn't a mother figure or decent parent. "You do realize, Brenda, that I could knock you down with one hand, and it would take a week for you to get up. I'm younger, fitter, and to be frank, smarter than you."

Brenda let out a loud laugh. "Trust me, bitch, I've taken on people far better than you." She started to raise her hand.

Logan grabbed her wrist. "You really don't want to do that."

"The hell I don't." She wrenched her hand out of the grip and made a fist.

"Brenda, stop," Taryn screamed. "Come on, Logan, she isn't worth your time or effort. Believe me, I learned that the hard way." She held out her hand. "Please, come with me."

Logan drew back her shoulders and snorted. "Goodbye, Brenda. Under normal circumstances, when I visit with my girlfriend's family, I usually say it was a pleasure. In this case, I hope you rot in hell." She shook her head and followed Taryn to her room.

In her room, Taryn looked at Logan, fearing she'd see disgust and anger. "I'm sorry that you had to witness that. I guess, I've lived with it for so long that it's the norm for me." She swallowed hard. "You have your truck now. I wouldn't blame you if you wanted to leave and get away from here as far as you can."

Logan pulled Taryn close. "Don't be silly. You're my girlfriend, and I want to be with you. More so right now. Did it hurt bad?" She touched a finger to the red mark.

"Not really. I think my skin is tougher there, it's her favorite target." She buried her head in Logan's shoulder and shuddered with emotion. "Am I really your girlfriend? Or, just a stop in the road like *she* said?"

Logan tilted Taryn's chin and smiled before placing a gentle kiss on her lips. "You are a breath of fresh air in my stagnant life. Do you think I'm going to let you go so easily? Besides, I gave you my phone. If you look, you'll see that it has my parents' number in it. Would I give you that information if I wasn't serious about keeping in touch? My mom would have a field day, if you called her and said I was just a fly-by-night lover." Logan chuckled.

"I have no point of reference, Logan. All I know is what Brenda has told me repeatedly. They take what they want and leave." She lifted a shoulder. "Would your mom really do that?" It was hard for her to believe that a mother would be anything other than what she'd lived with all these years.

"You betcha. My mom would love you and my dad too. He's a sucker for a pretty face. Much to my mom's chagrin. He says he never had the chance with the beautiful girl's, because he met my mom so early. They got married at eighteen. Mom, of course, just rolls her eyes. They've been married for forty years."

"You want me to meet your parents?" Taryn shook her head. "I find that hard to believe, Logan. We've just met."

Logan gently pulled Taryn closer to her chest. "I meant what I said about us getting to know each other better. For better or worse, that's my parents too. Are you okay with that?"

150

Taryn could feel the warmth beginning to fill her body. "Yes, I am." She began to cry. "Please say you won't go. It will be so lonely here without you."

"I have to go, but I promise, either I'll be back for you, or you can come to me. I just need to work a few things out first. Will you trust me?"

"Oh, Logan, I trust you with my life. No one has ever made me feel the way you do. If I have to, I will wait forever."

Logan laughed. "I hope it isn't that long." She kissed Taryn deeply then went to lock the bedroom door and put a chair under the knob. "Hmm, now, you mentioned something along the lines of pleasuring me." She grinned and moved so that their bodies were touching.

When Logan began slipping her hands under her T-shirt, Taryn shivered in anticipation. When the T-shirt and her bra came off, she thought her legs would give out.

"I've never wanted someone as much as I want you." Logan began placing light kisses over the exposed skin. "You are so beautiful." She picked Taryn up and laid her on the bed, then removed the rest of her clothes.

Taryn could feel herself floating on the high of Logan making love to her. Each kiss, touch, stroke, and murmured word of adoration sent her senses reeling and her body burning with desire. As Logan's lips explored further down her body, Taryn lifted her hips wanting, needing, craving the contact. Finally, Logan's tongue began lavishing her center, causing her to cry out at the incredible pleasure she was experiencing. "God, Logan please don't stop."

Snuggled in Logan's body, Taryn couldn't help the tears that began to fall.

"What's wrong?" Logan lifted her chin. "Did I hurt you?"

"No." Taryn ran a finger along Logan's cheek. "You make me feel so special."

"That's because you are, Taryn. You are the most special woman I've ever met."

"Thank you." Taryn pulled Logan close and gave her a deep searing kiss. Then she began a slow, passionate assault on the body of the woman she knew, without a doubt, she'd fallen in love with.

The next thing Taryn knew was that her alarm was going off. She kept her eyes closed, willing the offending noise to stop. If it stopped, then that would mean she didn't have to go to work and Logan wouldn't be leaving her.

Logan turned over and kissed her cheek. "Good morning, beautiful."

Taryn kissed her after wrapping her arms around Logan's neck and pulling her close. "I wish I didn't have to go to work and we could have a few more hours together."

"After I get all my things together, what do you say I come by the Tavern for some breakfast? We can say our goodbyes then."

"I'd love that. I—"

There was a loud banging on the door. "Get your sorry ass out of bed and go to work. Take that abomination with you. I want her out of my house. What I heard from you last night disgusted me."

Taryn rolled over on top of Logan and grinned. "Wanna fool around and make lots of noise? Bet that'll get her going."

Logan slid her hand between their bodies, and once again, they became one.

CHAPTER TWELVE

Taryn arrived at work with a smile on her face.

"Well, don't you look happy," Rosie said. "Did you have a good few days off?"

"I had the best days of my life, Rosie."

"Does it have anything to do with that good lookin' woman I saw you with Friday night?"

Taryn grinned. "Yes." Then she frowned. "She leaves today."

Rosie came out from the kitchen and engulfed Taryn in a hug. "Sweetie, if it is meant to be, it will be. Just 'cause she's leavin' doesn't mean she won't be back."

"Yeah, that's what she said."

Rosie pulled back some. "How'd Brenda take it?"

"Not well. Oh, Rosie you should have heard the things she said, right to Logan's face. It was horrible, and I was so embarrassed."

"Did you really expect anythin' else?"

Taryn shook her head. "No, but I hoped that she'd at least be civil."

Rosie let out a belly laugh. "Child, it is Brenda we're talkin' about, and I don't think she knows the meanin' of civil, unless she's tryin' to finagle a bigger tip."

Just then, the door opened and a brilliant smile filled Taryn's face. "She came."

The sight of Taryn's smile made Logan's heart take a roller coaster ride, and she walked quickly to her.

"You're here," Taryn whispered.

"Of course, I am. If I say I'm going to do something, I will. Never forget that." Taryn's bright smile had Logan's heart skipping a beat. *God, I'm going to miss you.*

"Did Brenda give you a hard time?"

"Never came out of her bedroom. I think I saw her at the window when I was leaving, and she gave me the finger."

Taryn laughed. "Sounds like something she'd do. Probably was too scared of you to come out and face you alone."

"I don't want to waste the time we have left talking about her. Can you join me for breakfast? I figure if I get on the road within the next hour, I can get home before the evening rush hour. Believe me, you wouldn't want to experience that in Chicago."

"How long does it take if you hit the rush hour?"

Logan chuckled. "I might get home in time to see the late news." At Taryn's shocked expression she smiled. "Not quite, but being stuck in traffic for more than thirty minutes is a nightmare. So, can you join me for breakfast?"

Taryn looked around the room. "Maybe for a few minutes. The breakfast crowd hasn't arrived yet."

Logan slipped into a booth and patted the bench. "Sit with me."

"Let me take your order first."

"Okay. I'll have the breakfast special."

Taryn nodded and hurried over to Rosie. Within a minute, she was sliding in next to her, coffee pot in hand and filling a cup. "I have five minutes, tops."

Logan ran her hand along Taryn's thigh and could feel the shivers her action caused. "You won't forget me, will you?"

Taryn brushed at her eyes. "Never." She rested her head on Logan's shoulder. "Thank you for coming into my life and showing me all the possibilities life can hold. I had no idea."

"I will be back." Logan could see doubt in Taryn's eyes, but there was something else. Fear. "I promise you, I *will* be back." She kissed the top of Taryn's head. "Trust me."

"I do."

"Order's up." Rosie bellowed from the kitchen hatch.

"I gotta serve the other table. Be right back."

Logan watched her go. *Damn. You deserve more than this, but am I the one that can do that?* Her thoughts were disturbed as the door opened and she saw six men walk in. *I guess this is it ...for now*. The next time she spoke to Taryn was when her breakfast arrived.

"Sorry, I can't stay and eat with you. The tables are filling up faster than I can get to them."

"Want some help?"

"You know how to wait tables?"

Logan laughed. "Of course, I do. For three summers that was my job."

"I can't ask you to do that. You won't get out of here on time, and you'll be stuck in traffic. I can't do that to you"

"Yes, you can. For you, I'd gladly sit in traffic. I'll eat my breakfast first then pitch in. Deal?"

Two hours later, the dining room cleared and Logan was finally alone with Taryn.

"Is there someplace we can go to say a proper goodbye?"

"Yes. Just give me a minute."

Logan watched her go over and talk to Rosie. When she came back, she took Logan's hand and led her to a small room off the main dining area.

"This is where they have private meetings. No one will be coming in here this morning."

Logan pulled Taryn to her and could instantly feel her body respond as their lips met. Soon, her hands were seeking supple, warm skin as they melted together. "Is there somewhere else we can go that is more private?" Logan asked, when the sound of voices echoed from the other room.

"I wish there was." Taryn buried her head in Logan's shoulder. "Rosie will probably come looking for me. She said she'd give me as much time as she could, but it sounds like this is it."

"I guess this is goodbye then."

"Not if you stay it won't be."

"Taryn, I need to go take care of some business, but when that is done, I will be back. I promise you that."

"Will you call me?"

"Every night." She winked, "Remember, I have your number, so you can't get away from me."

"Promise?"

"Yes." Logan smiled and kissed Taryn. A clearing throat had her looking at the door.

"Taryn, I'm sorry, but we have customers," Rosie said.

Logan reluctantly let go of Taryn. "Talk to you tonight."

Taryn nodded, and as she left the room, three whispered words floated in the cool air, "I love you."

Logan's stomach lurched, and she closed her eyes as the words pierced her heart. *Damn, I forgot to give her the present.*

†

Brenda sauntered into the Tavern and made a beeline for Taryn. "I see your dyke is gone. Boohoo, whose gonna lick you now?"

"Go away, Brenda, I'm working."

"Now that she's gone, you'll be the town dyke, lesbo, lezzy. Take your pick, they all refer to you."

Taryn moved within inches of Brenda. "I'd rather be any of those than the town whore like you."

The hand was so quick that Taryn didn't see it until her cheek stung. When a collective gasp circulated among the Tavern's patrons, Brenda glared at them and everyone immediately looked away. She snarled at Taryn, "I want you out of my house," before walking away.

"Bitch," Taryn said under her breath.

"So, didn't she like what you got her for Mother's Day?" Rosie asked with a grin.

"Wish it were that simple. I'm happy and have someone in my life besides her. I don't think she likes that."

"Do you really think she'll kick you out?"

"Who knows." Taryn bit her lip. "I doubt it. Who else could she get to rent out that tiny room?"

"Well, if she does, my place will be free."

"Thanks, Rosie, but I can barely afford to pay Brenda."

"I'd make you a good deal." Rosie patted her arm. "It's good to see you happy."

"She left."

"She's comin' back, right?"

"I hope so." Taryn looked at the cook and shrugged. "We'll see, Rosie. If not, then maybe I'll see about getting out of this town and away from Brenda. I think moving somewhere else would be good for me."

"Got an order for takeout," Bill Mayes, the day manager, said.

"Comin' up." Rosie smiled and walked away, leaving Taryn standing by herself. *I sure am gonna miss you, Rosie.* She saw a wave from one of her tables. *Back to work.*

†

As predicted, Brenda didn't throw her out. She did ask for the rent a day early, which meant Taryn would be living very frugally until payday. That didn't dampen her spirits though, since she and Logan had spoken for at least an hour every night since she left. It was Friday, Rosie's last day, and the sadness that filled Taryn was acute. She needed the connection with Logan more than ever and couldn't wait to speak to her. She looked at her watch. "Only three hours to go." She entered the house looking forward to the call.

"Well it's about time you got here." Brenda scowled. "You know my poker group is playing here tonight, and you need to get things ready for me."

Taryn blew out a breath. "I don't think so."

"Excuse me? As long as you live in my house, you'll do as I say."

"Not anymore, Brenda. I'm done being your lackey."

"How dare you speak to me like that." Brenda moved so she was standing toe to toe with Taryn. "It's that dyke, isn't it? She isn't coming back, so get over it, and go get things ready."

"She'll be back," Taryn said.

"Oh, sure she will. How would you know?"

"We talk." Brenda glared at her, and Taryn know she'd made a mistake.

"You've talked to her? Have you been running up my phone bill?" Brenda grabbed her wrist.

"Let go. No, I haven't been using your phone."

"Then just how did these supposed conversations take place? Are you a telepath now?"

Taryn pulled the phone out of her pocket and held it up.

"Where'd you get that?" Brenda demanded.

"She gave it to me. See, you're wrong. She *is* coming back."

"I don't think so." Brenda ripped the phone from Taryn's hand and threw it on the floor before stomping on it with her foot. "Now, go get things ready."

"I hate you," Taryn screamed while picking up the pieces off the floor. She hadn't thought to write Logan's number down. *How will I reach her? What'll I do?*

Brenda grabbed her hair and pulled her up. "I said, get things ready."

Taryn had a choice to make, and in that instant, she chose to stand up for herself. "Do it yourself." With those words, she turned and left the house.

†

She spent the night in the shed. Early the next morning, she crept into the house to get ready for work. She'd thought long and hard on how to get in touch with Logan, realizing that she really didn't know much about her. *Chicago is a big city.* Her plan was to go to the garage on her break and see if Tommy had a phone number for Logan. It was a start.

"Hey, Tommy," Taryn said to legs that were sticking out from under a car.

"Yeah, who wants me?"

"It's me, Taryn."

"Is your friend's truck having more problems?" He scooted out from under the car and looked up at her.

"No. My phone broke, so I don't have her number. I was wondering if she gave you a phone number."

Tommy got off the creeper and stood. "Let me go see. Did she leave town?"

"Yeah, she left last Tuesday."

Tommy pulled out a piece of paper from a pile. "Yeah, here it is. 312-993-1532."

Taryn felt her heart sink. That was the number of the phone Logan had given her. "Okay, thanks, Tommy." She started to leave then stopped. "Did she give you an address too?"

"Yep. Here, take the paper she filled out. All I need is the work order and what she paid." He held out the paper to her.

"Thanks." Her heart was happier now that she had some way of contacting Logan. As soon as her shift was over, she'd go back to the house and write Logan a letter explaining what Brenda did to the phone and why she hadn't answered any calls."

When four o'clock rolled around, Taryn waited impatiently for Brenda to show up for her shift. She'd been thinking all afternoon about what she'd say to Logan. She'd gone to McClean's General Store and spent her last twenty dollars on what Logan had called a burner phone. She would give Logan that number to call.

"Hey, where's your mother?" Bill Mayes asked. "If she doesn't show up soon, you'll have to take her shift."

"Don't think so. I've put in my hours, and I have plans for tonight. I'll go home and see what's going on. I'll tell her to hurry."

"You can't just leave me without help," Bill protested.

"Sure I can. My shift is over. I'll find her and tell her you're waiting on her."

"What about the customers?"

"Bill, you once waited on tables here, so you know what to do. She'll be here soon." Taryn took off her apron and handed it to him. "As I said, my shift is over."

†

On the walk home, Taryn just shook her head. Before Logan came into her life, she'd have kowtowed to Bill's demands. "Not anymore. No one is going to walk all over me, ever again." She walked up the steps to the house and went inside. Nothing prepared her for what she found. Brenda was lying on the floor.

Taryn began to shake. She held a hand to her mouth and let out a sob. She had seen her grandparent's bodies in coffins, but she'd never seen anything like Brenda lying there with her mouth open, looking waxen and cold. There was no doubt that Brenda was dead. "No," she cried. "What should I do?" She paced around the room, purposely not looking at the body. Taking a deep breath, she went to the phone to call 911.

In the distance, she could hear the wailing of sirens. Soon, Sheriff Waltham and the fire department volunteers would arrive. Taryn panicked. For the first time in her life, she was truly alone. Rosie had left, and although she hadn't been much of a mother, Brenda was at least a body. She looked at Brenda and shook her head. The sirens grew louder and then stopped. Taryn could see the flashing lights and knew that there'd be a crowd of people next.

Taryn mechanically opened the door. In swooped the sheriff, followed by five orange-vested men. Taryn stood trembling, while a tall man bent down to check on Brenda. He shook his head and stood. "We'll need a body bag," he said. A young guy she recognized from high school hurried out the door.

"Can you tell me what happened, Taryn?" Sheriff Waltham asked.

Dazed, Taryn looked at him then shook her head. "I don't know. I just came home from work and found her like that."

A gurney topped with an open black bag was rolled in, and Taryn watched in fascination as the five men lifted Brenda's lifeless body onto the gurney. She heard a zipper being closed and watched as Brenda's body disappeared.

"Take her to Doc Rogers and see if he can tell us what happened to her," Sheriff Waltham told them.

"I have no idea what to do next, Sheriff," Taryn said once the others left. "I don't have the money for a funeral either."

"Go see Kevin Richmond."

"The lawyer? Why?"

"I remember, back when your dad was alive, he told me that he and your mother went to see Kevin after you were born to make their wills."

"I had no idea. How will that make a difference?"

Ted Waltham put his arm around her shoulders. "Your dad and I were close, and he told me he wanted to make sure that you and your mother were taken care of, in case anything happened to him." He gave her a gentle squeeze. "Go see Kevin, and don't worry about the expense of a funeral. We have a fund for that."

"Thank you, Sheriff, I'll give him a call and set up an appointment."

"Is there anything else I can do for you, Taryn?"

"No."

"Okay then. Give me a call if you need anything, you hear me?"

"Yes, thank you."

He squeezed her shoulders once more before he left. Taryn heard him saying, "Move on folks there's nothing here for you." She hoped they did.

Taryn gathered a piece of paper, a pen, and an envelope and sat at the kitchen table. Pulling the paper that she got from Tommy out of her pocket, she began writing a note to Logan.

Dear Logan,

I haven't called you, because Brenda took the phone from me and broke it. I didn't know your number, so I got your address from Tommy and purchased another phone. My new number is 312-429-6231. Please call me. I need to talk with you. Brenda is dead.

Love,
Taryn

She sealed the envelope, put one of Brenda's stamps on it, and slipped it into her pocket. After looking out the window and finding no one lingering outside the house, she went out to the nearest mailbox and the lawyer. Darkness surrounded her, and she looked up at the sky. "Logan, where are you?"

CHAPTER THIRTEEN

After speaking with Kevin Richmond, who luckily was still in his office, Taryn walked back to the house with what she knew was a flabbergasted expression. Two months before her father's death, both her parents had made their wills. Each left everything to the other, and in the event of both their deaths, Taryn inherited everything. Kevin also informed her that her grandparents had left the farm to her, not Brenda. That was the biggest surprise of all. Had she known, she would have moved out there and away from Brenda.

She looked around the house. Everything was the same. Her eyes fell on the always closed door to the room that Brenda forbid her to enter. Brenda's room. With trembling fingers, she reached for the doorknob. She wasn't sure what she expected to find, but what she saw wasn't it. Everything was neat and clean. Those were not attributes that she'd give to Brenda, since the housework had always been Taryn's job.

She ventured further in, opened the closet door, and was immediately assaulted by the smell she associated with

164

the woman. Repulsed, Taryn took a step back. She noticed a safe sitting in one corner. She tried the handle and it didn't open. She looked around the room. "Where would she put the combination?" Her eyes fell on a wooden writing desk. Taryn sat in the chair and opened the side drawers on the left and right but found nothing. The center drawer was full of papers. She pulled them all out. Nothing. When she went to slide the papers back in, they caught on something. Taryn pulled out the drawer and found a small envelope taped to the left side of the drawer. "Found it."

With eyes the size of saucers, Taryn looked at the contents of the safe. There was a neat bundle of one hundred dollar bills, along with several documents that looked like deeds. A separate, small, manila envelope was labeled *poker*. Inside, Taryn found another large stack of money. "What the hell? This is unbelievable. Where'd *she* get all this?"

For the next two hours, Taryn went through the contents of the safe. The wrapped hundreds amounted to thirty thousand two hundred dollars. She did some quick math and figured that it was almost the amount she had paid in rent over the years. "So that's why the only bills she'd take were hundreds." For a moment, she wondered if Brenda had saved the money to give to her at some point, then discarded the idea. Brenda was a taker not a giver. The poker money amounted to almost three-thousand dollars.

"There might be enough cash here to put a new roof on the old house and fix the inside up some."

She continued to sort through all the documents and found some stock certificates for Apple and GE that her father bought when she was born. There were also some things called bearer bonds from 1980, but she knew nothing about them and set them aside. The deed to the farm that had her name on it was there too and she growled when she saw it. Brenda had kept something from her that she would have cherished. "Bitch."

On the bottom of the pile she found a letter to Brenda from her grandparents.

Dear Brenda,

Taryn is having such a wonderful time here this summer. Once again, she's asked if she can come and live with us. I think you should reconsider your stand on this. We can devote all our time to her, which you cannot, working all those late hours. I know you said you needed her to stay with you, because you needed the SS payment you got for her. We would gladly pay you however much that is if you'll just let her stay with us. Please, think about what is best for your daughter.

Your in-laws,
Doris and Ben

Scribbled in red below the letter were the words *no way in hell they are nothing but farm hicks.* She assumed Brenda wrote those words.

The phone rang. Taryn got up from the floor where she'd been sitting for several hours and went to the table by Brenda's bed. "Hello."

"Taryn, this is Ted Waltham, and I'm calling about your mother's autopsy."

"Okay."

"The doc determined that she died of a heart attack."

"Okay."

"Where do you want us to send the body?"

"I have no idea, Sheriff. I thought you told me you'd take care of that."

"I need to know your preferences, Taryn."

"Won't it be cheaper to have her cremated?"

"I think so."

"Then let's let her burn. She made my life a living hell, so why not..." Taryn sucked in a breath. "I'm sorry," she sobbed.

"How about a simple service at the church after the cremation?"

"I know, when my grandmother died, there was a meal afterwards. Will I have to do that?"

"No. I will arrange for coffee and cookies to be at the church. That will be enough."

"Thank you for all your help, sir."

"No problem. I'll call you when all the arrangements are made."

"Thank you." Taryn hung up the phone and finally allowed her tears to fall. All she had ever wanted was a mother that loved her. That wasn't Brenda. Now she was truly alone, and the one person she wanted to speak to was unreachable. She left the bedroom and went to her own, where she flopped down on the bed and cried into the pillow.

The next few days were a blur. Taryn attended the funeral, listening to the minister wax on about Brenda. He obviously didn't know her, or he wouldn't be saying what a kind, gentle woman she was. *He must have slept with her.* She looked around at those in attendance, recognizing a few and wondering who slept with her and who she played poker with. *Maybe it's all the same.* The sheriff had been true to his word and arranged everything, including the memorial cards and a guest register.

After the service, Taryn stood alone in the annex watching everyone that had come to the service chat among themselves. She had served most of the folks at the Tavern, at one time or another, yet none had offered their condolences.

"Taryn, please accept my sincere sympathy for your loss," Ted Waltham said, taking her hand. "I know you and your mother had a…tenuous relationship, at best, but she was family. We must make allowances for them from time to time."

Taryn nodded. "Thank you."

"I heard you quit your job at the Tavern. What'll you do now?"

"Don't know." She eyed the man. "I do know I'm not sticking around here for very long." Once she heard back from Logan, she'd decide what she'd do next.

"I can tell you from experience that you need to take some time before you make any decisions." He patted her shoulder. "I'll be around if you need me."

"Thank you."

When the sheriff walked away, Taryn's eyes widened. A line of people was waiting, apparently to speak with her. She shook hands with them and accepted their condolences graciously, all the while wondering who they were talking about. *Kind. Delightful. Sweet. Wonderful. Giving.* They weren't words she'd use to describe the woman that would hit her without any provocation. The woman who would demean and belittle her. Although she had a safe full of cash, Brenda had never once bought Taryn anything new. Every stitch of clothes that she had, including underwear, were hand-me-downs. She could still hear Brenda telling her, "They are clean and you'll wear them." The first thing Taryn did when she had her own money was buy new underwear.

The crowd finally thinned, and she let out a relieved breath when the last person went out the door. She was just about to leave, when the minister, a short and portly man, walked up to her holding out the urn. "You almost forgot to take this."

No, I didn't. I don't want it. "Oh, so I did. Thank you for the kind words you said about Brenda. Did you know her very well?"

"Oh, yes. We went to school together, and I dated her before she met your father."

"Really? Well, I need to get going." He pressed the urn toward her and she took it. "Good-bye."

Taryn walked down the street. A block from her house, she opened the urn and scattered the ashes behind her. Brenda would forever be a part of Bourne Falls. "Good riddance."

†

The next day, Taryn drove the convertible out to the farm to take inventory of what needed doing to make the house livable. Parked in front of the house, she could see that it would need a coat of paint along with a new roof. Out of the car, she climbed the three steps. They and the front door were usable but would need shoring up. Inside the house, she looked around, noting what needed repair in every room. Her great-grandfather had built the solid house. Although years of neglect had taken their toll, nothing was in such drastic shape that it needed complete replacement. The only room that needed remodeling was the bathroom.

She made her way to the barn and upon entering, she looked to her left as the memory of making love with Logan resurfaced. It had been a week since she sent the letter to her lover. Brenda's words taunted her. *You're nothing but a plaything to her. You'll never hear from her again.*

"She'll be back. I know it."

Taryn ventured farther into the barn before opening the door to what had been her grandfather's workshop. To her surprise, she saw that all his tools were still there. She'd be able to use them when repairing the house. "Strange that no one looted this place." Thinking about it more, she realized that the house hadn't been ransacked and it didn't look like squatters had lived there. "That is really bizarre."

Standing in the middle of the barn, she looked around and spied what she'd hoped to find. Her grandfather's old Ford truck. "Yes." All the tires were flat, but other than that, it looked good. She opened the driver's door and got in. *How many times did I sit in this seat while he taught me to drive stick shift?* She reached up, slid her fingers between the visor and the roof, and smiled. The keys were still there. "Now, for a miracle." Holding her breath, she inserted the key and turned it. Nothing. "Move on to plan B. Get Tommy to come out here, get the truck, and make it run again." Once she had a truck, she could start moving her things out to the farm.

Getting out of the truck, she saw another door and wondered if the contents were still there. The door creaked open when she pushed on it, and she smiled. All the boxes of her grandmother's things were still there. "Once I fix the kitchen, everything will go back in there just like she had it." She nodded and walked back out into the main barn. "First things first. I need to go find Tommy."

†

It had been a month since Taryn last heard from Logan. Brenda's words about Logan using her then leaving her were still replaying in her mind. Taryn made one bedroom livable and brought her furniture, along with the safe. She moved out to the farm, permanently. She'd had a new metal roof put on and had a handy man come out to repair lose floorboards and several windows. The rest she'd planned to do herself, only to realize she knew nothing about plumbing. Remembering that the sheriff had offered to help, she called him to ask if he could give her a hand with the bathroom. He readily agreed.

"Do you see how this fits on those bolts on the floor?" Ted Waltham asked.

"Yes, I can't believe it's that easy. I think I could do that myself now."

Ted, looked up and smiled. "Let's turn on the water and see if it leaks."

Once the toilet installation was complete, the sheriff looked around the small room. "That should do it. What's next?"

Taryn shrugged. "Well, I don't know how to hook the propane up to the stove, and the faucet in the kitchen leaks."

"Let me take a look."

They walked into the kitchen, and Taryn could see his eyes widen.

"This looks just like I remember it. You did a great job in here, Taryn."

"You've been in the house before?"

"Lots of times. Remember that your dad wasn't only my deputy but a friend too. Now, let's see about hooking up the propane."

An hour later, they had finished and were sitting at the table in the kitchen, drinking iced tea. "Looks like things are coming along." The sheriff smiled. "How much more do you have to do?"

"I have one bedroom floor to stain, and I need to remove the wallpaper and paint in the living room. After that, I need to find someone to paint the outside."

"That's a big job. If you want, I can ask around and get some names for you."

"Thanks, I'd like that."

Ted slid his chair back. "I'd better get going. I still need to mow the lawn at home."

"Thank you for all your help. When it's all done, maybe you and your wife would like to come for dinner." Taryn held her breath. She'd never invited anyone other than Logan to anything.

"I'd like that, Taryn. I'd like that very much."

†

With the bathroom and kitchen functioning, she began the arduous task of stripping the old wallpaper off the walls and applying a new coat of paint in what would be the guest bedrooms. She was washing out a paint brush when she heard a truck—*no it's more than one*—pulling up. Four pickup trucks, one was the sheriff's, came to a stop outside the window. Taryn hurried out of the room and out of the house.

"Hey, Sheriff, what's going on?" Fear that he was going to evict her made her body stiffen.

"Well, me and the boys are here to paint your house for you." He smiled. "If I remember correctly, the house was white with green trim."

"That's right. I didn't know this was happening. I don't have the paint, but I can go into town and get it." Taryn quickly went over the conversation she'd had with the sheriff. No, he hadn't said anything about painting the house. *He said he'd give me some names, that's all.*

"Got it, Taryn." Ted turned to the others. "Let's get the scaffolding set up and get those shutters off the windows."

Taryn, was stunned. She watched the men set about their tasks, and when Ted came up to her, she asked, "Why?"

"Because, that's what neighbors…friends…do for one another. Your dad asked me once to watch over you and your mother if anything ever happened to him, and I've been doing that ever since he passed. I couldn't do much about the way your mother treated you, but I could make sure you were safe."

Sudden realization filled Taryn. "That's why no one ransacked the house."

Ted only smiled. "I need to go help the others."

A warm feeling spread throughout Taryn's body, before a broad smiled curved her lips.

†

She had finished all the bedrooms and moved out to begin the front room, but it was getting dark. She'd put in a long day. "First thing in the morning, I will finish this room before moving outside." With a yawn and a stretch, she headed for a quick shower before going to bed.

Taryn woke the next morning with a smile, just as she had every day since she'd move to the farm. Once she got everything squared away with the inside of the house, she'd move outside and begin repairs there. "Then I think I'll get some chickens." With that thought came another smile, and she headed to the kitchen for a cup of coffee.

Taryn was painting the front room a light grey, when she heard tires on the dirt road. *Mail is early today.* She continued to paint till she heard the vehicle stop, and she laughed. "Must be *occupant* mail. Can't wait to see what that is." She heard a door close and looked out the window. "My god." Dropping the paintbrush, she rushed out the front door.

"Is it really you?"

CHAPTER FOURTEEN

Logan looked up at the grey building to the third floor where her apartment was. Nothing had changed. It was as she expected—still the same old same. Graffiti was on the lower level, and some smart ass had even reached the second floor. *Next, it'll be my floor.* Time to move on, her gran would have said. She slowly inserted the key in the lock and entered the small reception area leading to the elevators—no one was there. She checked her watch. It was three forty-five. *Damn, I made good time.*

Walking toward the elevator, bag in hand, she knew the first thing she was going to do was call Taryn. *Yeah, the beautiful, sexy Taryn.* In all her life, she had never met such a giving woman. The drive back had been an agonizing battle with the temptation to just say to hell with normality and return to Taryn.

Life wasn't that simple. *I've been burned before, taking a partner at first sight. If this is going to work, I need to know it will last.*

She jabbed the up button and immediately the metal doors opened. She entered and pushed the number three. The

174

doors slid shut. Leaning back against the cold surface of the metal box, a picture of Taryn's face came to mind. "I miss you, Taryn, and that shouldn't be, you know. To find someone who makes me feel like you do is a chance in a million…nah a zillion." Logan frowned. "I found you and I'm not letting you go." The elevator beeped, and the doors opened. "I'm not letting you go." She smiled in satisfaction and headed down the corridor to her apartment.

†

"Hey, how was your day?" Logan cradled her phone as close as possible to her ear and let out a soft sigh at hearing Taryn's voice.

"Sad, you left me."

"I'm sorry—" Logan began.

"No, don't feel guilty, Logan, I know you had to go. As much as I hate working in the Tavern, it's a commitment. You must have them in Chicago too. Still, it makes me feel sad that I won't have you in my bed tonight. I'm gonna be lonely."

Logan closed her eyes and nodded. "Same here. I desperately wanted to talk to you on my trip home, but I had no phone."

"Oh my god, what if you were stuck in an out of the way place—"

"Taryn, it didn't happen. I'm home and speaking to you. So, has Brenda been amiable, if not good?" There was a soft chuckle at the end of the line, and Logan's insides melted.

"Brenda could never be entirely good. We both know that. Let's see, she came into the Tavern, screamed at me before she slapped me…the usual."

"I don't like her hitting you. That's not what mothers do."

"Mine does. This evening, she's been less caustic than normal, which mean she wants something."

Logan sagged against the wall. "I'm sorry."

"Hey, it's precious time we have, so no more talk of Brenda."

"Good plan. What's on the docket tomorrow?"

†

Logan paced the apartment. Taryn hadn't taken her call the last five times she'd tried. They'd agreed about the time the night before, and now it was two hours later. *Is this it? Am I right not to give my heart so easily? Damn, what a fool. What if someone else has arrived at the Tavern, and she's being nice to them? How would I know if she's as innocent as she makes out?* The words in her head didn't match the heartache she felt, and she slumped to the floor in the hall. Cradling her head in her arms, she silently chastised herself for being a fool, as her eyes filled with tears.

When her phone rang, she threw off her morose thoughts and answered the call. "Taryn, I was worried about you—oh, Mom?"

Logan's body responded better than her brain, as she jumped up and became attentive to her mother's words. "Mom, I'll be on the next plane out of here. I promise. Yeah, I know, but you and Dad are more important. Sure, I'll text you my flight number. Mom, thank god that you're both going to be okay. I don't know what I'd do…yeah, I know, shut up and get on with it. I love you, Mom. See you tomorrow."

Logan was horrified knowing that her parents had been in a car crash. They were alive but had suffered injuries. They needed her help.

For a split second, she saw Taryn's face in her mind's eye and smiled. "You would understand that I have to go. I'll call you tomorrow and hope you pick up."

†

"Mom, it isn't rocket science."

Sara Perry frowned and waved at the microwave. "It is when you have your strongest hand in a cast. Let me tell you, this feeling of being inadequate is disconcerting. Your dad is worse, with his two broken legs."

"Mom, I'm sorry, I was preoccupied." Logan took the bowl of oatmeal from the microwave. "Here you go. Want me to pour in extra milk?"

"No, I can do that." Sara sat down at the kitchen table and stirred her breakfast then poured in a little more milk. "You've been here three weeks, and I've noticed something different about you."

Logan turned to her and frowned. "What?"

"Well, you never did tell me who Taryn was."

"Mom." Logan met her deliberate gaze. "You never asked, and she's…well it's…. Darn, I could call it complicated, but it isn't really."

Sara watched the frown on her daughter's face become a pained expression.

"I never asked, because I was more worried about your dad. His incapacity and being in a wheelchair has taken a hard toll on him. However, he's in good spirits today. His golfing buddies have taken him out for breakfast, which leaves me and you here alone to talk."

Logan shook her head. "Wow, my lucky day then."

"Don't be trite, Logan. Is this the one?" Sara watched Logan's bland expression remain the same. *Damn, that woman from college Logan professed to love has certainly done a number on her.*

Logan waved her hands around. "What do you mean *the one*?"

Sara chuckled. "She is. I know it. Why would you be so edgy? Did I tell you about when me and your dad met?"

"Yes…yes. Mom, enough of the speculation. Taryn is different. I'll give you that. I can't say she is the one though."

"Who are you kidding, love, me, or yourself? Anyway, when did you last call Taryn? Lovely name by the way."

"There are times when I hate you, Mom."

"Sure, you do. Most daughters feel that way about their parents. Nanna always said ignoring them was fatal." Sara chuckled, recalling her mother's interference with her affairs. She'd been right, most times.

Logan sighed heavily, and Sara smiled. *Let it go, love.*

"She's had such a terrible life, Mom. I think something really bad has happened to her or she would have answered my calls. I know it. We weren't lovers for long, just a long weekend, but it was important. I know it—for both of us."

Sara sucked in a deep breath, exhaled slowly, and grinned. "Lovers then, ah…not a conquest on your trip?"

"No! Definitely not."

"Good, I like that. Tell me about your Taryn." Sara sat back in her chair. Logan brought her coffee to the table and sat opposite her.

"Mom, she's so innocent and lovely…"

†

Logan stared at the phone clutched in her palm. She'd called Taryn so many times her dial finger was sore. The conversation with her mom had been cathartic, speaking about Taryn with someone other than her inner self. Her mom wanted to meet Taryn and get to know her. She placed the phone to her forehead for a second and groaned. "She can't meet her if I can't contact her. I wonder if that bitch Brenda has kicked her out of the house, or worse, hurt her." The thought of Taryn alone in that town, with no friends or someone to watch out for her, hit so hard Logan was sure her stomach would be bruised by the onslaught.

"What the hell do I do?" From some spark of sanity, she remembered the sheriff from Bourne Falls. "Now what was his name again…hmm, Wally no. Walter…damn think, girl. Waltham that's it Waltham." She pressed the button on her iPhone and asked Siri to locate the phone number for the Bourne Falls sheriff's office.

Minutes later, she was dialing the number and waiting for a response.

"Bourne Falls sheriff's office how can I help you?"

The voice was male but sounded young. The sheriff she'd met was an old man with a gravelly voice. "Hi, is Sheriff Waltham there please?"

"Sorry, the sheriff is on vacation and isn't due back in the office for three weeks. Can anyone else help? I'm Deputy Dan Daniels."

Logan bit her lip. "I'm trying to find the whereabouts of a friend of mine who lives in Bourne Falls. I'm worried. She hasn't contacted me in several weeks."

The deputy coughed. "I can try, but I'm just a temporary until the Sheriff comes back. Let me have her name."

"Taryn, Taryn Donavan. If it helps, she works at the Tavern." Every muscle in Logan's body tensed in anticipation.

"Sorry, I don't recall the name, but that doesn't mean she isn't a resident of the town. I'm on loan from Sanderson Cross, while the sheriff is away. I've only been here for a month, getting acclimated, before he left on vacation. Although I've met the people who work at the Tavern, I don't think I heard that name mentioned. What does she look like?"

Logan blinked several times, as Taryn's face floated in her mind's eye. For a moment, she was at a loss for words.

"Ma'am, did you hear my question? What does she look like?"

"Sorry, yes, yes. She's twenty-four. She has short chestnut hair, brown eyes, and flawless skin. She's about five five, slender, but not a stick."

"No, sorry. She doesn't work at the Tavern. Everyone there is at least thirty plus, or looks it. Hmm, maybe I shouldn't have said that."

"But that can't be." Logan gasped. "She was working there six weeks ago, when I left town. She would have told me if she was leaving. Does her mother still work there? Her name is Brenda."

"Definitely no Brenda that I recall. Are you sure you have the right town?"

Logan sighed and stared at the cream-painted wall opposite her. "I'm sorry I've wasted your time, Deputy. Thank you anyway." Tears stabbed at her eyelids for release. "Maybe I'll call when the sheriff gets back. He definitely knows Taryn and Brenda."

"Sure thing, have a great day." The call ended.

Logan's fingers gripped the phone tighter, until the pain made her release her palm along with the tears that streamed down her cheeks. "What has happened to you, Taryn?" She was about to make another request from Siri, when the door opened and her dad was wheeled inside by one of his friends.

"Hey there, love. Have you and your mom righted the world while I've been gone?"

The happy voice broke into Logan's misery and washed it away for the moment. She'd call the Tavern later. They were bound to know what had happened to Taryn. *Silly woman, that should have been my first call.* "Sure we have. Did you have a good time, Dad?" She brushed away the tears and smiled broadly, as she opened the door to the kitchen for him.

†

Logan watched her dad take several steps with crutches, the cast on the right leg had been removed and everything was looking up. His left was a worse injury, and it might take another two to three weeks before the cast could be removed. His wide smile told its own story. He was mobile again, even if only slightly. She shifted her gaze to her mom, who was smiling too. Her fractured wrist was healing, but still weak. Logan had stayed until her dad was more mobile.

She'd been there six weeks, and in that time, she had searched her heart for what she thought might have happened to Taryn. There were so many conclusions, it was hard to relate anymore. A part of her now wondered if that time in her life was a dream. A beautiful, exciting, sexual time, but not meant to be a reality.

She'd called the Tavern at Bourne Falls and was told, "Bitch left us high and dry, weeks ago. Now, unless you want to book a table, I'm busy." The angry man disconnected the call. Her instinct was to get on the next plane back to the closest town to Bourne Falls and find out what the hell was happening, but her parents needed her and they had to come first.

"Logan?" Her mom was walking toward her.

"Hey, Dad is doing great, and he looks happy."

"He is. And now, my love, it's time to make you happy. Take this." She handed her a manila envelope.

"What's this?" Logan squinted at the paper.

Her mom chuckled. "The only way to find out is to open it."

Tearing open the seal, she pulled out a piece of paper. Her eyes bulged. She waved the paper at her mom, both hands in the air. "I don't understand."

"Well, you always did take a lot of convincing. You've been pining for that girl from the moment you arrived, and you won't rest until you know what's happened to her. You'd better get your things together. I believe the flight takes off in four hours.

Logan stared at the e-ticket for the flight to Chicago. She pulled her mom into a hug and kissed her. "I love you, Mom. You didn't have to do this. I have money."

"I know you do, but you'll need it for that project you've been talking about."

Logan gave a strangled cry. "Only if Taryn is in my life…at least in that place."

"Then go find her, love. If she's half the woman you described, then how can she not want to be involved with my little girl?"

Logan raised her head and smiled. "Less of the little."

They both smiled.

"Off with you. It's going to take me an hour to get your dad back in the car. Now that he can move on his own steam, he won't want to be confined again."

Logan wiped away the moisture that was obscuring her view and rushed toward her bedroom. Her parents were simply the best.

†

The Ford Ranger pulled up at the placard that said *Bourne Falls Garage*. For Logan, this was déjà vu as she climbed out of the vehicle and headed to the open doors. The sound of tapping caught her attention, and she walked toward the noise. A Toyota Tacoma was in the garage pit, and Logan saw the crawler wheels under the vehicle. She peered down and saw legs. "Tommy?"

There was no response. She bent down and pulled at the crawler, "Tommy."

The crawler moved, and she managed to jump aside before it came into view.

Sure enough, it was Tommy. Logan saw his expression shift from annoyance to anxiety.

"Oh, it's you. Have you broken something again?"

"Yeah, it's me. Nope, Shelia is just fine. You did a great job." Logan decided being nice to this guy might get her what she wanted, or at least some information.

He wiped grease from his hands with a soiled rag and nodded. "What brings you back here? I know it isn't my handsome face."

If that was his idea of a joke, it was lame. "I'm looking for Taryn. The house looks like it hasn't been lived in, and she isn't working at the Tavern."

Tommy flexed his puny muscles and grinned. "Well, she moved. If you are such good buddies as everyone around town said you were, she'd have told you right?"

Logan balled her fists. *No use losing my temper, even if the weasel-faced man annoys me.* "I had to go away for a while. Do you know where she lives now?"

Tommy walked around the Toyota, obviously thinking he was in control of the situation. Logan sucked in a deep breath. *I will not throttle the life out of him. I will not.*

"Her mom died and she left town. Don't know the address. She got yours though. I gave it to her weeks ago."

Logan closed her eyes for a few seconds. Had Taryn followed her to Chicago, and she hadn't been home but with her parents? *Damn. Why hasn't she called?* She frowned. Things made more sense with his next words.

"She said that her phone broke and she didn't know how to contact you."

"I see." Logan turned away, her stomach diving to a painful, fathomless pit. "Thanks, Tommy." Where would Taryn go if she was alone? *Damn, the list is endless without the Brenda shackled to her side.* As she left the building, Tommy shouted something at her.

"I heard a rumor about a farm."

Logan's heart jumped in her chest. She turned back and ran over to Tommy and hugged him before kissing his cheek. "You are a life saver." She sped toward her vehicle, and a minute later she was heading out of town.

CHAPTER FIFTEEN

"Is it really you?"

Logan didn't hesitate as she ran the few feet between them, pulling Taryn into her arms. Words were irrelevant, as the warm vibrant body throbbed against her own.

"I can't breathe."

The hoarse words made Logan relax her hold, as she stepped away from Taryn's body just enough so she could see her face. "I'm sorry."

Taryn smile, her face peppered with specks of light grey. "No—it's okay—just a little tight, that's all. I can't believe you're here. How did you find me? When you didn't call, I thought you'd forgotten me."

Logan shook her head, as she stared into the brown eyes that looked at her apprehensively. "Never! I thought you'd decided that I wasn't good for you. I had no term of reference especially after you stopped calling me. I missed you so much." Logan crushed Taryn to her once again but not as hard.

"I wrote you after Brenda smashed up my phone. I asked Tommy for your address." Taryn sighed. "That was five weeks ago, and you never replied or rang my new number."

Logan kissed the top of Taryn's head. She whispered, "I never got your letter. I hadn't been home long when I got a call that my folks were in a car accident. I went directly there to take care of them." She shrugged. "I never went back to the apartment, so I haven't picked up my mail."

"Are they okay?"

The concern in Taryn's voice was the final piece in the puzzle of Logan's errant emotions. "They're getting there. My mom bought me the plane ticket back to Chicago to find you. I'm sorry about Brenda's passing."

Taryn pulled away. "Don't be sorry. I'm not. I found out things after her death that finally confirmed she didn't love me. Worse, she probably hated me."

Logan was about to speak what would have been a hollow platitude but Taryn continued.

"Logan, I'm my own woman now. I have the farm, and look, it's taking shape and…. Like you said, if you give people a chance, they might be better than you think. I found that they are. Sheriff Waltham has been spending some of his vacation helping me get this place livable, and he even brought some neighbors over to help. I finally have a place I want to call home, and I'm happy."

The pride and pleasure in Taryn's voice amazed Logan. She relinquished her hold and stared at Taryn, seeing not the naïve, almost childlike person she had first met but a confident woman in charge of her own destiny. The question was, would Logan be part of her new destiny. "I'm so happy for you." Logan looked at the farmhouse and saw the significant changes. "You are one talented woman, but then I always knew that." Logan smoothed down the sides of her jeans, unsure what to do or say next.

Taryn smiled. "Because of you." She waved her hand around. "All of this is because of you. You made me see that I could do things for myself, and I have. Do you remember Ken Stuart—"

"The guy who does metalworking and whose father knew your grandpa?"

"Yes. I'm going to go to his classes, and they start in two weeks. Maybe I can do more with that side of my life."

Logan's heart fell. *Am I too late? Has Taryn decided on a path that doesn't include me? Who would blame her after all these weeks of silence?*

"You don't think it's a good idea, do you?" Taryn asked.

"Absolutely, it is the best idea. I'm proud of you." Logan's insides felt as if Taryn, the innocent loving Taryn that she knew, was now a dream.

Taryn grinned. "Great, because if you are going to be part of my life, I want you to understand that there are some things we can't do together."

Logan's world righted in such a way she was euphoric. She moved the few inches between them and placed her hands gently around Taryn's face. "I love you. I'm happy if you are, in whatever you do." Then she kissed her.

When the kiss ended, Taryn took Logan's hand and began dragging her to the house. "Come on, I want to show you what I've done."

Logan smiled indulgently and happily followed Taryn up the stairs. "If the outside is anything to go by, the inside must be spectacular."

"Isn't it great? People I've only served food to, and didn't think they knew my name, came out here and helped with the exterior paint." She grinned. "Sheriff Waltham, Ted, has been so helpful. I couldn't have done all of this by myself. Now, the inside is mostly something I've done.

187

Come on." She took Logan's hand, pulled open the screen door, and guided them inside.

"Are you sure this is the same house?" Wide-eyed, Logan took in the front room.

"I've done all the upstairs bedrooms, and this is the last room I need to paint."

"Taryn, this is wonderful."

"Come on, I want to show you my...our bedroom. I hope you'll like it, but if you don't we can change it. No problem." Taryn took Logan's hand again and led her up the stairs. "It's down here." She pushed open a door and smiled. "What do you think?"

Logan slowly surveyed the room. The first thing that caught her eye was the king-sized bed covered with a beautiful, hand-stitched, patchwork quilt. The colors were vibrant, and she walked closer to the object and touched one of the patches—it was the picture of a house—this house. "Wow," she whispered. The green pastel walls each bore one of Taryn's metalwork pieces, including the wonderful dragonfly she loved from her old home. The floor was a lovely, maple hardwood, polished so that you could almost see your reflection. Turning, she smiled at Taryn who appeared apprehensive. "This is marvelous. Did you make the quilt too?"

Taryn laughed. "Quilting is something I never learned, but my grandmother did it when they first moved to this house." She stepped closer to Logan and put her arms around her. "You're really here, aren't you?" The kiss, at first, was gentle and full of promise but soon ignited into a burning inferno. She grabbed at Logan's T-shirt and had begun lifting it over her head, when a car door closed in the driveway. "Who the hell can that be?" She went to the window and looked out. "It's Ted. I forgot he said he'd be by today with some of his friends to paint the barn."

Logan laughed and pulled her close. "Then let's not disappoint the guys. I want to thank them for helping you out. We can wait. Trust me, we have the rest of our lives to be together in every way, starting from now." Logan kissed Taryn again, and her heart pounded at the way their bodies seemed to meld together. Now that she came to think of it, it had always been that way. "I love you."

"I love you too. I like the idea of having the rest of our lives together."

†

Logan pulled Taryn closer, as they snuggled on the sofa in the living room. The men had left as dusk set in. The barn was taking shape, and it amazed her how a few helping hands could turn something derelict beautiful again.

"You're quiet...anything wrong? Was it that phone call you took earlier?" Taryn whispered and placed a tender kiss on the side of Logan's neck.

Logan smiled and held Taryn a little tighter. "Nope, nothing is wrong at all. In fact, it couldn't be better. I have some news from that phone call."

Taryn turned and faced Logan directly. "And?"

Logan chuckled and gave Taryn a feather-light kiss. "Do you remember that coffee shop in Sanderson Cross?"

"Of course, I do. Why?"

"Ah well, I've been talking to Sally and..." Logan winked then grinned.

"Oh, come on, Logan. You can't leave it like this, it's mean." Taryn scowled.

Stroking a finger over the creases of Taryn's face, Logan said, "Want to go into Sanderson tomorrow morning? I'm going to see Sally and sign a contract of sale, but if you don't want—"

189

Taryn flung her arms around Logan. "You're going to do it? You're going to start your own café here, well not here, but—tell me all about it."

Laughing, Logan eased the excited woman away from strangling her. "Well, I knew from the first moment I saw the place it was for me. When I saw your reaction as we looked around, it took all my self-control not to make an offer right then and there. I got a sweet deal for the café, including the equipment, and I paid a little extra for the back lot with the barn. I figured that could be your studio, and you could sell your pieces from there. I guess that might be a dumb idea, now you have your own place."

"A dumb idea? I don't think so. Thank you for thinking of me. I can't think of anything better than to work alongside you." She shrugged. "We could live here. It isn't that far to Sanderson from here. What do you think?"

"Wherever you live, that's where I'm going to be. We could use the upper floor of the café as a stock room or maybe let it out. I guess meeting was a catalyst for both of us, because for the first time in my life, I'm happy about what the future holds. That all comes down to you." Logan placed her hands around Taryn's face and kissed her slowly. When they broke apart, she whispered, "Thank you for coming into my life and loving me."

"Trust me, Logan, you saved my life." She ran a finger along Logan's cheek. "When I cleaned out Brenda's house, I found she had a safe. Inside was more money than I could ever imagine. Will you let me be your partner in the café?"

Logan frowned.

"You don't want me as your partner?"

The panic in Taryn's voice made Logan blink rapidly. She hadn't been expecting that offer. "I'm just surprised that's all."

"Surprised that I have money, or surprised I want to be your partner in the business." She bit her lip. "I guess it was too forward of me to ask something like that. I'm sorry."

"No, no don't be sorry it's just…crap, I'm not saying this at all well. I'm glad you have money and your mother finally gave you something for all those wretched years you had with her. It's just that you have this place and the land as well. I guess…I'm just being foolish…. Sure, we can do that. I want you as my partner in all things." Logan smiled.

"I understand that the café is your dream just as this place is mine. What about if you buy half of this place and I buy half of the café?" Taryn laughed. "Brenda would be rolling in her grave if she had one." She took Logan's face in her hands. "I love you and want to spend always with you."

"Let's seal that deal with a kiss. Shall we? Now, exactly where did we leave off earlier…?" Logan kissed Taryn, and began to snake her fingers under Taryn's shirt to touch the skin her body had been craving to feel for weeks. *I'm home*, her body and mind agreed in that moment.

EPILOGUE

The music was loud and the laughing louder. Logan, beer bottle in hand, stared out over the porch rail of their home. The farm had been a great place to settle down, separating them from their business interests in Sanderson Cross. She sighed. "Damn, I can't be any happier. Who could be?" Her eyes tracked the woman who had made her life complete. Grinning, she watched her lover sitting between her parents engaged in what looked like an animated conversation. Taryn waved and Logan echoed the action.

Two years ago, she had been a footloose person with no prospects for the future, at least none that appealed to her. Now, she had a wonderful partner who had married her that afternoon. *How the hell did I get so lucky?*

"Hey, as the bride, or is it the groom.... Hell, who cares? What are you doing here all alone?"

Logan smiled at the craggy features of the one man who had been hell bent on making sure that their life together went better than it might have. Neighborly acceptance was the word around here, and most folks agreed. "Hi, Ted. Are you enjoying yourself?"

"Damn right, I am. Daisy hasn't stayed any place this long since…well, last month when we came over for dinner. She loves you both. You know that, right?"

Logan shrugged. "You both love us." She winked. "Besides, my parents would never invite you to their place if you didn't."

Ted chuckled. "Your parents are grand. You know, I think of Taryn as…well, a surrogate daughter. We were never blessed, and I know it took a long time to show but—"

Logan placed a hand on the sheriff's arm. "It was meant to be this time. I'm a great believer that people come into one's life for a reason. Some stay a short time, others the whole of our lives, because they're family. But when we choose that special stranger to let into our lives and K-pow fireworks flare, no matter how short or how long we have with them, it's the right thing."

Ted shook his head. "When did you become a philosopher?"

Logan touched his arm. "No philosopher, just a very grateful woman who found a woman who chose to love me unconditionally." Her eyes found Taryn, who was laughing, and her heart swelled with love.

"Then take my arm and let's go and chat with the most beautiful woman here."

Logan grinned as she shook her head. "Daisy won't be happy to hear you say that."

Ted laughed. "You going to tell her? Besides, today, Taryn is the most important and beautiful woman. Right?"

"Absolutely god damn right. No offense, Ted, but I think I can do this without help." Logan placed her beer on the railing and headed for her wife.

It took longer than expected to walk over to the side of the barn, as several of the neighbors stopped to congratulate her. Eventually, she caught a break and sidled up to the back of Taryn's chair. She rested her hands on Taryn's shoulders, and the most amazing smile greeted her. "Hey, you look happy." Logan smiled slowly.

"I am, believe me, I am. What about you?" Taryn's gaze never wavered.

"Happiest day of my life, except…"

Taryn rolled her eyes. "I hate you when you don't finish the sentence."

Logan chuckled and winked. "Sure you do. That's why you married me, right?"

Taryn shrugged. "Okay, what's the exception?"

Logan bent her head as close as possible to Taryn's ear. "The day I met you." She heard the distinct inhale of a deep breath and saw tears forming in her wife's eyes. Tenderly, she stroked them away. "My mom is the only one who can cry today, okay? Not my special girl."

"I know you just got married and all, but you do have other company."

Anyone else who said that would have ended up with a black eye, but Logan snared her dad in her sights. "Yeah, Dad, I know. I guess I should have considered that before inviting everyone here." She draped her arms gently around Taryn's shoulders and looked at her parents. "So, what was the conversation about? You all looked excited from the porch."

"Oh nothing, love," Logan's mother replied quietly.

Taryn moved slightly and turned to look at Logan. "Your parents are worried about me going to New York next month. All alone in a big city kind of thing."

Logan nodded. "Understandable. Bet you reminded them you were a big girl now and could manage the Big Apple."

"Sure, I did. Besides, I won't be alone. Ken is going with me. It's his friend's gallery."

"I'm so proud of you, darling. I always knew that if given the chance people would flock to your art. In fact, I think I said that from the first moment I saw your creations." Logan grinned. "Enough of this speculation. There's music, food, and drinks. Let's really get our party started." Logan held out her hand. "Would my wife care to dance with me? It's been all of half an hour since I last held you in my arms."

Taryn jumped up. "Try to stop me," she said, taking the hand offered.

"Come on, Mom and Dad, I know you've both been itching to dance, so let's go."

There was a grumble or two, but they sprang up like spring chickens and followed the newlyweds to the makeshift dance area in the barn. As they entered, a crescendo of applause greeted them. The country music stopped, as Logan nodded to the DJ. The guitar intro to James Arthur's song, "Say You Won't Let Go," drifted into the building, and Logan pulled Taryn close. "This was the song that was playing when I entered Bourne Falls. I guess fate struck at that moment, because I own every word of this song when it comes to you."

Taryn smiled. "Guess I do too. It was what I asked you before you left."

"Our song?"

"Our song." Taryn pulled her closer and kissed her softly. "I'll never let you go, ever. You do know there is another song that reminds me of you."

Logan frowned. "Really? What?"

"Addicted to You." Taryn gave her a saucy smile.

"Whoa, that song is next, and I'm pretty sure my parents will freak."

Just then, Jack, Logan's father, tapped her on the shoulder. "May I have this dance with my new daughter?"

Logan smiled. "Of course, Dad."

"You really think of me as a daughter?" Taryn asked.

"Of course. You married into the family, and that makes us your parents. Is that okay with you?"

Logan saw the tears in Taryn's eyes. "Oh, yes…yes…yes." She held a hand over her heart. "A wife and parents all in the same day. Life is wonderful."

Jack kissed Taryn's cheek. "Shall we?"

Logan's heart swelled at the sight, and her eyes misted. In that moment, she knew her life was complete.

†

Sated after their first lovemaking as a married couple, Logan's hands splayed across Taryn's stomach as she slept. She smiled, recalling their final quests. Mary Dixon, soon to be Mrs. Davy Randal, pushed and pulled a stumbling Davy to his car before they left the property. She and Taryn had played matchmaker about a year ago. Somehow, dinner at the farm, instead of their usual interaction at the Tavern, had been a catalyst to a romance. So much so that Mary was pregnant and the baby was due in three months. Logan glanced down at the peaceful expression on her wife's face. Bubbles of happiness threatened to burst out of every pore of her skin. How weird—wonderfully weird—that the mundane and annoying event of Shelia breaking down had changed her life forever. That's exactly what happened when the woman in her arms had come into her life.

A smaller hand captured one of hers, dragging it to warm, supple lips before placing a kiss there. The action drew her focus to her wife. Taryn stretched and turned in her arms. Her firm breasts pressed close to Logan's, and a shiver of anticipation coursed through her.

"Penny for them?" Taryn placed a gentle finger to her temple.

Logan grinned. "You can have them for free. Besides, they were mostly about you."

"Only most of them? Oh, I'm gutted." Taryn chuckled, her finger tracing a path down Logan's cheek to her lips. Logan captured the digit in her mouth and sucked. "God, that makes me wet," Taryn said.

Logan released the flesh and pulled Taryn closer and kissed her hard. When they came up for breath, she whispered, "I love you." She watched the slightly dilated eyes of her wife and the heavy breathing. "Too much for you, huh?"

Taryn shook her head, before commencing her own exploration of Logan's mouth. Nothing was sacred. Minutes later, or it could have been hours, they broke apart.

"God, I certainly did create a monster, didn't I?" Logan stared deep into Taryn's glazed eyes. "I'm so damn lucky."

Taryn giggled and nestled her head into Logan's shoulder. "Yeah, you are."

Logan sucked in a silent breath at that simple statement. When she had first met Taryn, and for many months afterwards, Taryn's self-worth was totally demoralized by her mother. That kind of comment wouldn't have entered her thoughts. "Good job that I married you then. I can't have you leaving me for a younger woman, especially when you become a celebrity."

Taryn stiffened in her hold and murmured, "Never going to happen."

"Never is right, my darling. You are mine for now and always. However, the celebrity part might now be out of your hands."

Taryn's expressive eyes captured hers. "It won't change anything between us, will it?"

Logan saw that kernel of insecurity. In fact, she felt the same. It was going to be a new challenge for them both. That was the key word—both—they were traveling the path together.

"It might. If you sell your work for ridiculously extortionate prices, we can buy the burger joint across from the café." She grinned. "You know, they've been going downhill since we set up there."

"You always know what to say so I don't feel bad. I love you."

Logan smiled slowly then gently turned Taryn and gently settled her body on top of her. "While I have breath in my body, I will never let you feel bad about yourself." She gave Taryn a gentle kiss and smiled. "Now, stop talking and let me love my wife."

The End

ABOUT THE AUTHORS

JM Dragon

JM Dragon is a New Zealand citizen, living in the beautiful Canterbury countryside. She loves to garden, travel, write, take care of her animals and family, and pursue her business interests—Affinity eBook Press and a Canterbury manufacturing company.

She is a keen reader of sci-fi, crime/mystery, classics, and romance, which help to feed her imagination for her own stories.

Currently published by Affinity eBook Press NZ LTD, her books include *The Promise*, *Do Dreams Come True*, *Fix-it Girl*, *In Name Only*, *The Destiny Series*, *Circus*, and 2015 GCLS winner *The One*.

You can contact her by email at:
jm1dragon@yahoo.com
or on Facebook at:
http://www.facebook.com/julie.dragon

Erin O'Reilly

Erin O'Reilly is an accomplished author with twenty-three published works, including her newest collaboration with JM Dragon *Take Me as I Am* and *Ready for Love*. She was the Sapphic Readers Award winner for her book *Deception*. Her focus as a writer is to develop strong characters that make a dramatic impact on her storylines.

When not writing, she is the Technical Director and CEO of Affinity eBook Press.

Contact Erin at:
erinoreilly@affinityebooks.com

OTHER AFFINITY RAINBOW BOOKS

For the Love of a Woman by S. Anne Gardner
In a world where oil is supreme, passion rules reason and there is always the threat of civil war. In this jungle of power Raisa Andieta resides as one of its masters. Her only desire is to rule it alone. Carolyn Stenbeck is just trying to keep her marriage together. Her only desire is to be able to escape and never look back. When Raisa and Carolyn meet, it is like fuel and fire…A storm is brewing. Civil War is in the air, and passion like the coming storm begins to erupt.

The Bee Charmer by Ali Spooner
After the death of her father, Nat St. Croix needs to decide on which direction her life should take. Does she continue her life alone, as a trapper and trader, or does she start over and try to fit into a town surrounded by strangers? Will the call of the wild and all that is familiar or, will the call of love capture Nat's heart?

The Organization by Annette Mori & Erin O'Reilly
The feisty, fiery women from *Asset Management* are back for another heart-stopping adventure! This time, their sights are set on a new mob boss Leonid Petrov. Val is tagged as the

go-to member to infiltrate Leonid's inner circle. Tasked with keeping Leonid's impossible new wife, Gina, safe, Val encounters more problems than solutions. Will wild card Gina be Val's Achilles heel and lead to her demise, or will it fill her with a strength she didn't know she had?

Jeager's by JM Dragon
When your world turns upside down and all your safe secure yearnings are thrown to the wind what happens? What would you do? University lecturer Dr. Kirsten Van De Pelt shortly due to retire early from her academic life is about to find the answers to those questions when Corley Anders, a TV star, enters her life. Will Kirsten take an opportunity of a lifetime or simply settle for the safety net that has been her life?

Running From Love by Jen Silver
Sam Wade returns home from a business trip to discover her wife, Beth, left her for another woman, Lydia. To take her mind off the break-up Sam accepts an assignment to learn to play golf at the newly opened Temperley Cliffs Golf Resort in Cornwall not knowing that is where Beth and Lydia plan to go too. There is more than one way to run from love; from never having to make a commitment and say those magical three words, "I love you." Find out what happens when they find themselves together—sport, betrayal, jealousy, and love form an unforgettable fusion of emotions.

Specter of Fear by Erin O'Reilly
Anne and Bailey are in love and planning a future together. Only the letters that Anne keeps getting are filling her with fear and doubt. Could the love they share really be a sham? Or is there something more behind the letters? Is the sender of the letters after Anne, Bailey or both women? Find out in this suspenseful tale…or is it a real story?

Back in the Saddle by Ali Spooner
The crew from *Cowgirl Up* is back in the saddle for more fun. In their new adventure, Coal, Stormy, and Gene get the chance to be part of something they have always dreamed of—a cattle drive. Even without the gang being at the MC2 ranch, there's still plenty of action going on with a new addition, Doc Bo, who brings a hint of jealousy and maybe the start of a new romance. Pull on your boots and hats, and hold on tight as you ride along with the crew of the MC2.

Faith in Rayne by Dannie Marsden
Welcome back Rayne and Lisbet from *Rayne Comes to Town* and *Rayne's New Beginnings*. Their life has flourished since meeting. Rayne ventures to Telluride, Colorado, where both adventure and trouble land at her feet. Lisbet heads to Telluride to reunite with Rayne, her head filled with dreams of their future only to have her dreams come crashing down. Can she find the strength to fight for Rayne, allowing her faith to guide them back to their love?

Ruined by Ali Spooner
Kade, a seasoned battlefield soldier has had enough, refusing to fight for greed. Now on a quest to return to her homeland she meets Iza. Iza, a slave from the army defeated by Kade, begs the warrior to take her on as a servant. Kade, sympathetic to the slave's request, allows her to travel as a companion and a friendship begins to form.

Refractions Trilogy by Angela Koenig
Follow the adventures of Rhodes Scholar Jeri O'Donnell who becomes embroiled in Ulster's fight for independence from Britain. Later Jeri travels through the Himalayan

highlands where she meets Kelly Corcoran, a tourist from the United States. Kelly is willing to gamble her heart, as Jeri struggles against involving anyone in her perilous and chaotic life. For Jeri, the true battle is confronting her attraction to violence as she struggles against losing herself in the exhilaration of combat.

Fortunes by Alane Hotchkins
Despite the curves life has thrown Remmy Garrick, her life is going along pretty good. Running her father's construction company fills the void left after the death of her lover. State Investigator Kira Kirpatrick is assigned the case, and meeting Remmy, a beautiful and alluring woman, is the last thing she wants or needs. Does Kira have the courage to step up and accept the love Remmy is offering, or will she continue to hide behind her secrets and let them control her?

Captivated by Annette Mori
Juliet Lewis has one too many quirks for her own well-being. Snooping was bound to get her in trouble. Sexy police officer Tanner Sullivan gets Juliet's attention and she wants to know more. Will Tanner turn out to be her jailor or savior? Sparks fly when the obsessive-compulsive Juliet and the paranoid Tanner cross paths in this quirky thriller with a new twist around every corner.

Pausing by Renee MacKenzie
Jordy Chapman is the Emergency Service Coordinator at Cypress Haven mental health facility in Naples, FL. Keira Yeager's family owns an upscale furniture store in Naples and orchestrates a generous donation of furniture to Cypress Haven. When the two meet, they hit it off immediately. Will

a Yeager family's anguish and misunderstanding threaten their new relationship?

Breaking the Silence by JM Dragon
Still grieving five years after the death of her father, Dilana Sterling is a shadow of the woman she once was…a successful author with a string of best sellers, and a longer string of women. Rachael Alderman, a teacher at the local orphanage, lives a quiet, yet satisfying life. When Dilana and Rachael meet, they develop a friendship that leads them on personal journeys of self-discovery. Will their memories of the past prevent them from moving towards each other, or will they find a path that leads to each other so they can experience life together?

The Termination by Annette Mori
Codee is having a bad day and it's only going to get worse. Sawyer, a compassionate young woman, is resigned to her fate. Her only question is what fate is that? After slipping on ice, Codee wonders if she is hallucinating and fallen into an Alice-type rabbit hole. The only thing she knows is that she needs to save Sawyer. Enjoy this satirical romance, with all of its twists and turns, that just might make you go, hmm...

The Next Time by Erin O'Reilly
What if you had the chance to make history stop repeating itself? Would you sacrifice today for a chance at a better tomorrow? There is a moment in everyone's life that defines their future. For Jac and Carol, that time is now. Jump ahead twenty-five years and meet Carol's granddaughter Livvy. She is ready for a challenge and is fleeing the nest and getting on with her life. Read this wonderful love story that spans several lifetimes.

E-Books, Print, Free e-books

Visit our website for more publications available online.

www.affinityebooks.com

Published by Affinity E-Book Press NZ LTD
Canterbury, New Zealand

Registered Company 2517228